CW01496239

THE
LONG DELAYED
REVENGE

Esther & Jack Enright Mystery
Book Ten

David Field

SAPERE
BOOKS

THE
LONG DELAYED
REVENGE

Published by Sapere Books.

24 Trafalgar Road, Ilkley, LS29 8HH

saperebooks.com

Copyright © David Field, 2025

David Field has asserted his right to be identified as the author of this work.
All rights reserved.

No part of this publication may be reproduced, stored in any retrieval system, or transmitted, in any form, or by any means, electronic, mechanical, photocopying, recording, or otherwise, without the prior written permission of the publishers.
This book is a work of fiction. Names, characters, businesses, organisations, places and events, other than those clearly in the public domain, are either the product of the author's imagination, or are used fictitiously.
Any resemblances to actual persons, living or dead, events or locales are purely coincidental.

ISBN: 978-0-85495-693-7

CHAPTER ONE

Hertfordshire, 1899

Esther Enright stood to the side of the small schoolyard of Cassiobury House as caretaker Stanley Pilgrim rang the handbell to summon the seventeen children back from the school grounds they had been playing in.

The Primary One class taught by Esther consisted of eleven pupils aged between five and eight years of age, including Esther's own daughter Lillian, or Lily as she was usually called. Primary Two had only six pupils, aged nine or ten, and their class teacher was the headmistress and proprietor, Emily Allsop. There were at present only two classes, and everyone in the small and elite private school knew each other well.

'All right, children,' Esther announced once they had formed up in two lines and fallen silent, 'since the weather is fine, Miss Allsop has granted permission for us to practise our Chestnut Dance once again. If you perform it as well as you did on Monday, then for your next rehearsal, as a special treat, you can all wear your costumes.'

There were several happy cheers, and a beaming smile of pride from eight-year-old Lily. Both the design and assembly of the 'human chestnut' costumes had been her achievement, under the guidance of Esther, who had once earned a precarious living as a seamstress before meeting Lily's father Jack, then a police constable and now a chief inspector at Scotland Yard, in charge of recruitment for the Metropolitan Police.

On an instruction from Esther, the pupils took up their dance positions. While ten-year-old Florence Cummings piped out a medieval madrigal in clear melodic tones, the pairs of dancers moved backwards and forwards, round and round in the routine that had become second nature to them over recent weeks. Esther smiled as she watched their hard work coming to fruition, and reflected yet again on her good fortune.

After bringing four children into the world, and watching her husband Jack progress in his chosen career, Esther was finally fulfilling her ambition to become a qualified teacher. She'd previously worked as a teacher's assistant at the Barking Board School — initially to preserve the peace between Lily and her younger brother Bertie. They had always been fierce sibling rivals, and the continuation of their friendly, yet mutually challenging, antics had threatened to disrupt the learning of the rest of the class, and Esther had been recruited to maintain order between them.

This had broadened into wider responsibilities that included actual teaching, given the shortage of accredited teachers for what had been a rapidly growing local primary school. Enjoying her new role, Esther had undertaken teacher training at a nearby college whose principal at the time, Emily Allsop, had recognised Esther's natural talent and invited her to join her as her second-in-command when she purchased Cassiobury House, a private school that Emily had ambitions to revive and expand.

Esther was fortunate in having a husband who both supported and encouraged his wife in her ambitions. Jack Enright had progressed remarkably swiftly in his police career, to a rank that very few ever attained, and certainly not at the age of thirty-two. He had generously agreed to move out to Watford with their family and into a house at the entrance to the Cassiobury estate, the ancestral property of generations of Earls of Essex. In recognition of its origins, the house was still called The Lodge, and came with a staff cottage for their two domestic servants, the cook Polly, and all-purpose maid Alice. Jack travelled to and from New Scotland Yard on Victoria Embankment by way of a train from Watford Station to Euston, and his office-based duties allowed him to be home in time for the family evening meal.

Of their four children, only Lily and Bertie, now aged seven, were of school age, but since Bertie's somewhat boisterous personality would not be an asset to Cassiobury House he attended the local Board School, where his behaviour was described as 'lively but respectful'. The remaining two children, four-year-old Miriam and three-year-old Tommy, were supervised daily by Polly and Alice.

Once the rehearsal was over the two classes returned indoors, where the rest of the afternoon was occupied in normal school activities. Once classes ended for the day, Esther took herself up to Emily's private rooms on the first floor for their usual weekly get-together to discuss school matters.

'I watched the rehearsal for the dance from the window,' Emily told Esther as she poured them both a cup of tea. 'You really have done a wonderful job. I have high hopes that those attending the fair will be encouraged to ask more about the school when they see how well the pupils behave.'

'Thank you,' Esther replied, 'and let's hope that you're right.'

Emily had purchased the school just over a year ago, hopeful of turning its fortunes around and increasing the pupil roll. The previous proprietor had died three years previously, leaving the business in the hands of two spinster daughters who had no interest in it, and a somewhat lacklustre headmistress who had allowed educational standards to slide to the point where the school roll was only a fraction of what it had been at its height, and had then resigned.

The school had been put on the market at a bargain price, and Emily had seized the opportunity to both acquire the school and employ Esther as deputy headmistress — the most natural teacher she had ever encountered. Esther had been both flattered and astonished at the offer to work alongside her former mentor, and shared Emily's hope that the establishment could not only be saved, but also restored to its former prominence. However, it took much longer for a school's reputation to be rebuilt than it did to lose it, and it was proving to be an uphill struggle.

'I have received enquiries this week from two local worthies who are interested in sending their children to us,' Emily told Esther. 'One enquiry was from the parents of twins, so here's hoping. I invited them to join us at the fair, so it's crucial that the school be seen at its best. Anyway, how goes Primary One?'

'Very well, all considered,' Esther replied. 'I'm obviously fortunate to have my own daughter in the class, since she can always be relied upon to give me an honest account, and she tells me that on the whole the pupils are enjoying what they're learning. There are one or two who seem to be struggling a little, particularly Tommy Brailsford, whose reading and writing are both below par compared with the rest of the class, and of course there's Annabelle Pickering, who always seems happier sitting at the back and contributing nothing. Lily's befriended her, more out of a sense of charity than anything else, I imagine. She assures me that Annabelle's reticence is borne of shyness rather than any lack of desire to contribute to the overall class effort, so there's hope even for her.'

'Annabelle's father was enquiring about her progress,' Emily said with a frown. 'I crossed my fingers behind my back and assured him that she's progressing as well as the rest of the class. He complains that she's withdrawn and "sullen" — that was his word — at home, and I rather think he's relying on the school to draw her out of herself a bit.'

'It's a pity that we can't tell parents the truth — that their children's performance at school is directly related to the amount of support they receive at home,' Esther commented.

'If we told them that,' Emily replied, 'we'd have no pupils left at all. Parents expect schools to perform miracles, as you know.'

'How are things in Primary Two?' Esther asked.

Emily inclined her head in a gesture of indecision. 'As the French say — *comme ci, comme ça*. Having only six pupils in the class is obviously an advantage. I'm pinning my hopes on the fair — some of the leading citizens in the county will be there, paying court to the Earl of Essex, and some may well have offspring who they wish to see educated to the level at which they might be suitable for entry into a profession.'

'Provided that they're boys,' Esther said with a grimace, 'but don't get me started regarding the closure of the professions to women.'

'I wouldn't dare,' Emily replied with a grin. 'Anyway, if there's nothing else to report, congratulations again on your magnificent achievement with the Chestnut Dance.'

Light of heart, and buoyed by Emily's appreciation of her efforts, Esther left the school and accompanied Lily as they walked the few paces down Park Avenue in the late afternoon sun until they reached its junction with Rickmansworth Road. Pausing to allow two wagons to trundle past in opposite directions, and holding firmly onto Lily's hand, she looked up at the glow of the sunlight on the upper turrets of The Lodge across the road. Jack would be home for the evening meal in due course, but before then she would be reunited with her remaining children, and supervise their games before dinner. She was happy and fulfilled, and once again gave thanks to God for all her blessings.

A few days later, Esther and Emily herded the children into the shade of a massive oak tree to one side of the cordoned-off section of the front lawn of Cassiobury House, to protect them from the powerful sun, and to prevent their costumes from wilting.

In front of the house itself had been erected a platform, and on it, smiling down on the sizeable crowd that had gathered for the fair, were two men and a woman. In the centre was the current occupant of Cassiobury House, George Devereux de Vere Capell, 7th Earl of Essex. It had been the earl who had first encouraged boys to kick a football around in his grounds, claiming that it was valuable 'manly' exercise for those he hoped to recruit into the Hertfordshire Yeomanry, in which he was a major. In due course those boys had become the founder members of what became the West Hertfordshire Football Club, which last year had amalgamated with its former rival, Watford St Mary's. It was this auspicious milestone in the development of professional 'soccer', as it was now called, that was being celebrated today.

To the earl's right, beaming graciously, was his second wife, the American heiress and socialite Adele Grant, whose much-needed wealth had preserved the estate from imminent bankruptcy, and was funding the fair. To his left was the man who had been hired to organise the fair, showman Henry Beaumont, who had risen from modest endeavours promoting local fêtes to become one of London's most successful music hall entrepreneurs. He had undertaken the organisation of the fair for a token fee, being eager to add a peer of the realm to his list of satisfied clients.

On a prompt from Beaumont, a man to the side of the cordon rope banged on a gong, and as the crowd fell silent the earl stepped forward and gave the speech he'd memorised for the occasion. It began with thanks to those who had 'taken the time to join us in celebration of a momentous step forward in the gentlemanly art of soccer,' followed by predictable self-congratulation on having been the original benefactor of what was now a thriving soccer club. There were glowing references to 'the support and encouragement of my dear lady wife' and 'the organisational genius of the proprietor and managing director of Beaumont Entertainments, who has generously given of his time to present a suitable array of entertainments for your delight and delectation.'

There was an opening paradiddle from a drum hidden away to the side, then two estate employees pulled back a section of the cordon and into the centre display area marched the 1st Battalion of the Hertfordshire Yeomanry, preceded by their pipe band playing a jaunty march, and with a uniformed captain at their head. After completing several circuits of the grass square, the soldiers in their khaki uniforms came to a halt in front of the platform. Their captain saluted the earl, who returned the salute with a beaming smile. Then the columns marched proudly off to the popular 'Black Bear' retreat melody, and the assembled crowd clapped appreciatively.

Next came a family of acrobats who regularly graced the boards of Beaumont music halls. In their spangled leotards, they cartwheeled and performed handstands, finishing off with a human pyramid whose topmost member, a child of six years of age, bowed solemnly to the party on the platform to rousing applause from the crowd.

While they had been performing, Emily and Esther had been lining up their 'Chestnut Dancers', checking that none of them was feeling faint or nauseous, and ensuring that none wished to visit the 'convenience tents' that had been erected discreetly under the trees.

'This next display,' the earl announced, 'comes from the children of Cassiobury House School, and consists of a traditional English folk dance that they've been perfecting for several weeks. So, under the guidance of their teacher, Mrs Esther Enright, please welcome the Cassiobury House Dance Group.'

The dance went perfectly, and the crowd, inevitably containing proud parents, cheered and demanded a repeat performance. A grinning Esther was only too happy to oblige. As she led the children off the grass and back under the oak tree to congratulate them on their 'proud achievement', she looked across the field to where Emily was chatting enthusiastically to a group of prospective parents. Then, as promised, Esther herded her young charges towards the ice cream tent for their well-earned reward.

She was joined a few minutes later by Emily, who congratulated her warmly on the children's performance, then announced that three sets of parents had made appointments to visit the school with a view to their own children joining at the start of the autumn term.

As the youngsters gleefully consumed their vanilla cornets, each topped with a cherry, Esther looked over Emily's shoulder as two men approached them.

'It looks as if the earl himself is intent on congratulating the school on its performance,' she told Emily, 'along with his acquaintance, Mr Beaumont. Perhaps we'll be asked to perform at more fairs in the future.'

Emily turned to look and her face paled. She whispered hoarsely to Esther, 'I have to go — please see that the children get back to the school safely.' Her head bowed low, she walked off at high speed.

CHAPTER TWO

'Assistant Commissioner Bruce would like to see you, when it's convenient, sir,' announced a uniformed constable.

Jack Enright sighed, pushed the monthly report on 'Recruitment and Manpower' within the Metropolitan Police to one side, and replied, 'I'll make it convenient now.'

Upstairs, Bruce looked up from his own paperwork and waved Jack into the seat in front of his desk. 'How's your report coming along?' he asked.

'I was halfway through it, sir,' Jack replied.

'How many more officers have we lost?' Bruce asked.

'Three more this week,' Jack replied. 'It's hardly surprising, given the circumstances.'

'All the same, we need to be more selective — or perhaps purposeful — in the matter of who we allocate to Whitechapel, Shoreditch and Bethnal Green. No mummy's boys.'

'I don't think any of the recent resignations were from mummy's boys, sir,' Jack told him. 'I think it's more a case of the increased workload, which in recent times has led to a cancellation of rostered days off and annual leave.'

'We can't help the fact that we're experiencing a new crime wave in the East End,' Bruce observed.

Jack couldn't resist correcting him. 'Our role is surely to *deter* crime, sir, so if it's increasing, then we're not doing our job.'

Bruce made an exasperated noise. 'You sound like those damned newspaper people who keep demanding to know what they pay their rates and taxes for. And assuming that you're right, then having less bobbies on the streets can't be helping.

Do you make sure that the ones whose initial allocation you're responsible for are sent where they will be most comfortable?'

'The only ones who'd be *comfortable* in the East End would be prize-fighters, sir,' Jack replied. 'And of course I've been careful in assigning those with a more middle-class background to stations such as Westminster or Bow Street, since I'm well aware that it was my own similar background that made me suitable for recruiting a "better class" of man into the service.'

'But *you* started out in the East End, didn't you, Jack?'

'Whitechapel, yes, sir — at around the time of the Ripper. But, as I already pointed out, the sheer workload wasn't as high as it is now, with all the gangs that seem to have taken over down there. It's sapping morale, and the constables, however tough they may be on the streets, still value their time at home with their families, and don't take well to being spat on in public while out shopping with their wives and children.'

Bruce considered this for a moment. 'I'd like you to go down there if you would, and sound out the reasons for the drop in retention numbers in those three stations I mentioned. We seem to be losing men faster than we're recruiting them. That's no criticism of you, Jack, I assure you — you're doing a marvellous job of bringing them in. But now I'd like you concentrate on retaining them.'

'I think I've given you the reason for the increase in resignations, sir, and I'm sure I won't get any other answers if I go down there and ask in person.'

'Perhaps not, but your presence, at your elevated rank, may help to raise morale. And while you're down there, I'd appreciate a report — just between ourselves, you understand? — on how bad this recent crime spree has become.'

'Yes, sir,' Jack replied through gritted teeth. The last thing he needed was to listen to dozens of *Why did you talk me into this miserable career?* complaints.

'Before you go, Jack, how's your uncle faring in his retirement?'

Jack's Uncle Percy, the man whose career in the Met had originally inspired Jack's own decision to join up, had retired a little over a year ago, at the rank of Detective Inspector. They had once worked together on a series of investigations that had made Percy a by-word in the force for getting results by not necessarily following the Procedures Manual, and Jack had only narrowly escaped being tarred with the same brush.

When not at work, Jack and Percy had maintained social contact through the regular family Sunday lunches at the family home in Barking, in which Jack and his sister Lucy had been raised. The tradition had been started by their mother Constance, and kept up by Jack and Esther for a while after Constance had died and they'd inherited the house. However, since the move to Watford, that regular contact had been lost, and Jack missed the company of Percy and his wife Beattie — who had taken Jack into their Hackney home after his father died when he was fourteen.

'To be honest, sir, I haven't seen him for several months now,' Jack admitted. 'Since the move to Watford, it's not been so easy to organise family gatherings, although I should imagine that Percy is hiding from my aunt behind his rows of runner beans in his extensive vegetable garden.'

'Well, give him my warm regards next time you catch up with him,' Bruce said, 'and tell him that my working life has become almost boring without the frequent reprimands that I was required to administer to him.'

'I'll be sure to do so, sir,' Jack replied politely, refraining from adding that the need to reprimand Percy for bending the rules to breaking point had often been accompanied by congratulations on catching another particularly nasty offender.

The East End could well do with the presence of Percy Enright, or someone like him, right now, Jack reflected as he took the stairs back down to his office.

'It's not the same as it was in our young days,' Inspector Preedy told Jack glumly from across his desk in Leman Street Police Station, the hub of H Division, responsible for policing Whitechapel. 'I still remember when you and I shared beat duties, and all we really had to do was move prostitutes from out of doorways, and break up the odd pub fight with our billy clubs. The prostitutes in those days worked for themselves, for a few pennies up a back alley — these days they've got "minders", and if you try to move them on you're likely to get a knife in your ribs.'

'I've heard that crime in the East End is now more organised, by gangs,' Jack said, 'and I'm here to learn more about how they operate. If we can break up the gangs, then presumably policing duties can return to what they once were.'

Preedy sighed heavily. 'If we could break up the gangs, Jack, then we could probably also stop high tide in the Thames. There seems to be no end to them — we bust one lot and then along comes another, waiting to take over. Imagine a garden in which new weeds pop up just as soon as you've pulled them up out of the ground. It's never-ending, and they seem to be getting the better of us.'

'So it's not just a few local criminal families, like it used to be?' Jack asked, to a vigorous shake of the head from Preedy.

'From Russia, mainly — or, at least, a part of it called Moldova. They claimed to have been escaping persecution, but once here they started forming gangs, supposedly for their own protection. Then, while no-one in Scotland Yard was looking, they realised that they had enough muscle to run the show. Prostitution is only one side of their enterprise — they've got a few unlicensed pubs that close down as fast as we raid them, then start up again the next night. Some of those pubs are used to stage cockfights and wrestling matches in which big money crosses the counter in wagers. They've recently taken to standing over local shopkeepers, threatening to burn down their premises if they don't hand over a share of the week's takings, and they're not above daylight robbery at knifepoint, either. A boot repairer in George Yard actually lodged an official complaint and two nights later his shop was torched. He and his family were living above the shop, and although they escaped the flames, they were beaten to a pulp by a gang waiting outside for them to run into the street. Funnily enough, we haven't had any more official complaints — just angry protests on street corners because we can't guarantee the public's safety any more. And the officers get abused, even when they're out of uniform. Some of them are so fearful for their own safety, and that of their families, that they're calling it a day and taking whatever other work they can get.'

'I've heard of a gang called the "Bessarabians" who were running the show up in Bethnal Green. Have I got that name right?'

'Yes, except here in Whitechapel they call themselves the "Stop at Nothing Gang". Russians, like I told you. There's a rival lot who call themselves the "Odessians", although recently they seem to have moved further north, into Hoxton.

Even the old local teams like the "Whitechapel Mob" and the "Bethnal Green Mob" give the Russian lot a wide berth.'

'As you probably know,' Jack replied thoughtfully, 'Scotland Yard has for some time maintained a specialist team known as the Special Branch that investigates political subversion of various kinds. If I could persuade someone high up in the Yard to appoint a new specialist team dedicated to breaking up organised crime gangs, do you think it would have any hope of success?'

'It couldn't do any harm,' Preedy conceded, 'but my experience has been that the senior types at the Yard don't want to admit that we're losing control down here.'

'Maybe not publicly,' Jack agreed, 'but the type of organisation I have in mind would operate in secret.'

'If they're going to be secret,' Preedy replied, 'then how can they do their job and assure the public that they're actually tackling the issue?'

'That'll be for me to determine,' Jack said, 'assuming that I can get someone to listen to me in the first place.'

That morning, Esther walked through the front gate of Cassiobury House in company with Lily to find several children standing in a morose group around Emily Allsop, all of them gazing up at something above the front doors. As she got closer, Esther could see the words *Lady Anne will take a child* daubed in red paint on the wall.

'Who's Lady Anne?' asked seven-year-old Clarissa Culshaw.

'No-one. It's just nonsense by some naughty person,' Emily replied when she finally found her voice. 'I shall go inside immediately and call for a constable.'

Esther escorted the children into their classroom, then told them to copy out words from their writing primer, while Emily made use of the school's telephone in order to call the nearby Watford Police Station.

Emily then summoned caretaker Stanley Pilgrim from his residence — a hut in the grounds to the rear — and Esther joined her briefly outside.

'Assumin' it 'appened last night,' Pilgrim said, 'I were in me bed by nine o'clock.'

'So you neither saw nor heard anything?' Emily asked.

He shook his head.

'And can you get it off?'

He looked up at the paint with a doubtful expression. 'I'll need ter get some turpentine an' use a scrubbin' brush.'

'Well, do that, please,' Emily instructed him, 'but not until after the police have seen it. I've sent for them, and they should be here shortly.'

As it turned out, it wasn't until ten-thirty that a young, fresh-faced and somewhat diffident-looking constable appeared in the small playground, invoking excited curiosity from the pupils. Esther was supervising the mid-morning playtime, and walked over to him. She recognised the same open-faced expression that she could still recall on Jack's face when she had first met him during the Ripper investigations, and instinctively tried to put the man at ease.

'Good morning, Constable,' she said. 'Are you here to investigate our graffiti?'

'Don't know about that, Missus,' he replied. 'I was told that someone had been writing on your wall.'

'Yes, as you can plainly see,' she replied, nodding towards the large red words.

'And who did it, Missus?'

'We've no idea, Constable,' Esther replied with exasperation, 'which is why we called you in to investigate.'

'But if you don't know who did it, then there's nothing I can do, is there?'

'You mean to tell me that someone can daub messages on a school wall in red paint, and you won't do anything about it unless we actually saw the culprit doing it?'

'Well, what do you suggest, Missus?'

'Ever heard of "making enquiries", Constable?'

'That's what I'm doing now,' he replied, apparently seeing nothing to be gained by making any further enquiry beyond asking, 'Who's Lady Anne?'

'I haven't the faintest idea,' Esther replied, adding sarcastically, 'but I'd be willing to wager that she wasn't the one who wrote on the wall.'

'I'll make a note of her name, just in case,' the constable offered as he extracted his notebook and pencil, leaving Esther open-mouthed in disbelief.

'So that's it, is it?' she demanded, hands on hips. 'That's the extent of your enquiry?'

'Like I said, Missus — unless you can point me towards who was responsible, my hands are tied.'

'Right up your back, by the look of things,' Esther huffed. 'Since you found your way in, you can presumably find your own way out!'

'Unbelievable!' Emily responded when Esther told her of her unsatisfactory exchange with the officer during their lunch break. 'Your husband's a police officer — isn't there something he can do?'

'I doubt it,' Esther replied dismally, 'but I can always ask, I suppose.'

It was unfortunate that Esther chose that same evening to tell Jack of the events of her day, with particular emphasis on the unhelpful response of the local police to the somewhat ominous message painted on the school wall. After a day spent being told of the crime wave being waged by gangs in the East End of London, the vandalism of a school wall in Watford seemed a mild affair, to say the least. But Jack could tell that the matter was important to Esther, so he agreed to call in at the local police station after supper, and at least register a protest at the lack of a positive response by the local constabulary.

It was dark by the time he presented himself at the front desk of the large police building at the junction of King Street and Smith Street, where a bored-looking sergeant raised his eyes reluctantly from his newspaper and enquired, 'Yes?'

'I'm here to see what investigations have been instigated regarding a case of criminal damage to the front wall of the Cassiobury House School, of which my wife is the deputy headmistress,' Jack told him.

The sergeant sighed, fumbled through a pile of papers on his desk, and eventually replied, 'Constable Jeffrey reported that someone had written something in red paint — something to do with a "Lady Anne".'

'And?' Jack asked.

'And what?'

'What are you doing about it?'

'What did you have in mind?'

'I thought perhaps an investigation into who is guilty of it.'

'The lady who Constable Jeffrey spoke to was unable to name the culprit,' the sergeant told him in a tone that suggested that this was the end of the matter.

'Is your Inspector still on duty?' Jack asked tersely.

'We don't have one at present. Inspector Bradley retired two months ago, and his replacement's a sergeant in St Albans. We *do* have a constabulary superintendent, though, and you can write to him at our headquarters in Hertford.'

'I will do that — you can depend upon it,' Jack assured the sergeant as he departed in an even fouler mood than he'd been in on his arrival.

CHAPTER THREE

Two days later Esther was relieved to see that as the result of considerable effort on the part of caretaker Stanley Pilgrim the daubings on the stonework were almost invisible. When Emily and Esther met for a cup of tea during a mid-morning break in which Pilgrim had been left to keep an eye on the lively and noisy youngsters in the yard, Emily was able to add something by way of a background to the message.

'I contacted the local historical society,' she told Esther, 'and they were able to cast some light on the "Lady Anne" referred to in the graffiti that Mr Pilgrim has succeeded in almost completely removing. I can only hope so, anyway, since I have some prospective parents arriving tomorrow afternoon, at around three o'clock. Can you ensure that Primary One are engaged in something suitably impressive, while I have Primary Two playing rounders on the grass?'

'Of course,' Esther assured her, 'but tell me about Lady Anne.'

'Well, it seems that the school building was erected on the site of an original Tudor manor house, before the Essex family moved in. It was apparently a Royalist house that was invaded one night by marauding Roundheads on their way out of London to engage King Charles's forces at Naseby. They did the usual pillaging, slaughtered a few retainers that they found inside the house, then violated the lady of the house — Lady Anne, of course — and made off with her only child, who was never seen again.'

'How horrible!' Esther muttered. 'Thank goodness we live in more civilised times. So, I suppose the reference to Lady Anne *taking* a child is a muddled version of the original event, since the truth is that she *lost* one?'

'That didn't stop the bucolic tale-weavers,' Emily replied. 'It's seemingly become embedded in local legend that Lady Anne's ghost may be seen in and around this place, seeking a child to replace the one that she lost.'

'So whoever daubed those words on the front wall knew about the legend?' Esther surmised.

Emily nodded. 'So it would seem, although I hardly suspect the members of the historical society. But if it's become a local ghost story, then anyone could have become aware of it.'

'At least we know the origin of the warning, and can write it off as local tittle-tattle,' Esther observed, but Emily frowned.

'Perhaps you and I can, given that we're both educated and rational,' she countered. 'But what about those who aren't? Local parents in particular, I mean.'

'One would hope that any prospective parents of Cassiobury House pupils are themselves both educated and rational,' Esther responded, to a knowing grimace from Emily.

'At this moment, quite frankly, I'd welcome *any* new parents, educated or otherwise.'

'What you are suggesting is completely out of the question,' Assistant Commissioner Bruce said hotly as Jack attempted to argue in favour of opening another covert department within Scotland Yard.

'Apart from restoring what passes for peace and quiet in the East End, and demonstrating to those moaners in the press that we *are* a worthwhile use of public money, we'll retain the manpower in stations such as Whitechapel, and those to its immediate north,' Jack postulated.

'And at what expense?' Bruce countered. 'Do you have any idea how much the Irish Branch and Special Branch cost us annually? I know that you and your uncle once achieved great results in identifying the means by which guns were being run into the country for the benefit of the Fenians, but you have no concept of how much it costs in manpower and utilities to engage in luxuries such as covert departments. Putting down criminal gangs is a job for local uniforms.'

'Which they aren't achieving,' Jack reminded him. 'You sent me down to the East End to investigate how we might turn around the rapid loss of men on the ground, and I'm reporting back that standard policing simply won't do it. The criminal gangs have too strong a grip over the local communities — they're terrorised to the point that uniformed constables are seen as the enemy. We *have* to attack the problem by covert means.'

'Such as?' Bruce challenged him. 'So far you've argued for the establishment of a covert department without specifying how it would set about ending the spree of a bunch of renegade criminal gangs.'

'If I knew all the answers,' Jack pointed out, 'I wouldn't be arguing for the establishment of an elite group who *do* know those answers. I've come up from being a uniformed bobby on the beat to someone who *manages* uniformed bobbies on the beat — I can't be expected to demonstrate a familiarity with covert tactics that aren't in the Procedures Manual.'

'Your uncle certainly had that talent,' Bruce reminded him.

'And if Percy Enright were still on the force, we wouldn't need to have this conversation. He was born to break the rules, which would have made him perfect for scuttling these gangs, using techniques which senior Yard officers would not approve,' Jack retorted.

'But he's *not* here, so let's look at realities. I can't justify launching a whole undercover department in the hope that in due course they'll come up with some stratagem to eradicate a new generation of organised criminal gangs.'

'But, sir —'

'But nothing, Jack,' said Bruce, cutting him off. 'Let it rest, and get back to recruiting enough numbers to replace the ones we're losing.'

Jack muttered to himself all the way back to his office, then threw himself into the chair behind his desk with a ferocity that threatened to disassemble it. He was reminded of an old problem he'd been called upon to solve during mathematics classes at Barking Grammar — if bathwater was going down the plughole at one rate, while the bath was being filled from the tap at another rate, how long would it take for the bath to become empty?

The reality was that it would never be completely empty, because there was always water coming in, but that didn't prevent the bath becoming utterly useless for its intended purpose.

It was Wednesday morning, the day the parents of several potential students were due to visit the school. As Esther walked up Park Avenue towards Cassiobury House with Lily by her side as usual, she rehearsed in her mind the word game she'd devised to keep the children of Primary One both happy and seemingly in pursuit of learning when the parents were shown a class in session. Her reverie was interrupted by Lily.

'Mama, why is Sarah Nesbit walking the wrong way?'

Esther looked up, and sure enough one of her brighter Primary One pupils was walking away from the school, back down Park Avenue towards Rickmansworth Road.

'Good morning, Sarah,' she said. 'Did you forget to bring something this morning?'

'No, Mrs Enright,' Sarah replied politely. 'Miss Allsop says that school's closed until after the lunch break.'

Esther quickened her pace and turned into the school yard, where an anxious Emily was pacing up and down with a pained expression on her face. She left Lily at the front gate with strict instructions not to move from there as she joined Emily and enquired as to the reason for her unprecedented action.

'The water's somehow been cut off *and* the lavatories are blocked,' Emily explained. 'Today of all days! I've sent for several plumbers, and it's to be hoped that at least one of them arrives without delay, because I can hardly welcome potential parents to a school that has no functioning lavatories, can I? I don't suppose you know any local plumbers prepared to treat us as a priority, do you? I can ill afford the expense, but I have no option.'

'What about Mr Pilgrim?' Esther asked, but Emily responded with an exasperated noise.

'He claims that it's beyond his ability to fix. "Proper buggered" were his exact words; seemingly the main sewer outlet is blocked, while the water supply's been cut off at the mains.'

'Is there anything I can do to help?' Esther asked, to a wry smile from Emily.

'Do you list plumbing among your many talents?'

By eleven o'clock they were speaking to a local plumber who was gleefully inserting a five pound note into the top pocket of his workman's shirt. 'It were all too easy, ladies,' he said. 'The sewer outlet 'ad some old rags stuffed in it, an' the input ballcock fer the water were glued so tight I 'ad to 'it it with me 'ammer a coupla times, that were all. Shame ter take yer money, but I will anyroad.'

'We're really most grateful to you,' Emily said, 'and if we need a plumber in the future, I'll be sure to send for you.'

As he cycled away, five pounds richer for less than a quarter of an hour's work, Esther looked enquiringly at Emily.

'If it was that simple, why couldn't Mr Pilgrim have dealt with both of those problems?' she asked. 'I'm obviously no plumber, but even so…'

'More to the point,' Emily replied, 'how did those problems arise in the first place, just when we needed the premises to be as pristine as possible ahead of the visit from those parents this afternoon? It's almost as if it was deliberate.'

'Well, things like that don't happen by accident, and certainly not both at the same time,' Esther replied as a thought occurred to her. 'How well do you know Mr Pilgrim?'

'He came with the school,' Emily told her. 'The previous headmistress hired him a few years ago, and from memory he came with excellent references. I have them somewhere in the papers I inherited when I took over. Perhaps I should be enquiring of those who supplied them.'

'I'm inclined to agree,' said Esther, 'but for now we need to concentrate on this afternoon's all-important event.'

The children had all returned by one o'clock, one of them bearing an indignant note from his mother: *If you intend to cancel school lessons for half a day in future, some advance warning would be appreciated.* Esther wrote a hasty reply for Emily's approval, then gathered Primary One together. 'We're going to play an exciting new game,' she told them.

By the time that three sets of potential parents were ushered into Esther's classroom, that game was well under way. She'd prepared a series of coloured cards, and the aim of the exercise was for the pupils to name a word that began with a given letter of the alphabet. If a pupil chose correctly, they received a yellow card. Once they'd collected ten yellow cards they could exchange them for a blue card, then when they had ten blue cards they could exchange those for a red card. The first pupil to collect ten red cards would then receive a prize of a pencil holder with the school's name embroidered down the side — another proud product of Lily's efforts with needle and thread.

'It went splendidly, and thank you *so* much for your inspirational effort with Primary One,' Emily enthused later as she and Esther sat around the teapot in her upstairs apartments. 'Mr and Mrs Bartlett will almost certainly be enrolling their twin daughters Mary and Rose for the January term, and Mrs Trusgrove, although a widow, hopes to persuade the trustees of the family trust of which she's the main beneficiary to authorise an advance payment of next term's fees for her son Christopher. You'll get the twins in Primary One, and Christopher Trusgrove will be joining Primary Two, where he'll be the second oldest in the class.'

The celebrations were short-lived. The following morning Esther arrived as usual with Lily to find eight-year-old Clarissa Culshaw sitting on the front steps, sniffling into her handkerchief. Lily ran across to comfort her, and after acknowledging her pride at having such a caring daughter, Esther asked Clarissa what was bothering her.

'It's the ghost, Mrs Enright,' she sobbed. 'I don't want it to get me. I'm scared to go into class, past that awful door down to the basement where she's buried.'

'What utter nonsense!' Esther replied instinctively, then reminded herself that to an eight-year-old the prospect of encountering a ghost was far from nonsense, so instead she tried reassurance. 'There's no ghost here in Cassiobury House,' she insisted, but Clarissa shook her head.

'There *is*, Mrs Enright — David Porter told me all about it when he met me on the way in this morning. She's a mother whose child was stolen by some bad soldiers, who killed her and buried her in the basement, and she's back to get her revenge by stealing a child from the school.'

'Why would she be wanting to take revenge on the school?' argued Esther rationally. 'If she's after revenge, then surely it would be against those soldiers who killed her?'

'But she wants her child back,' Clarissa moaned, 'and it was a girl, so David says. She'll come for a girl.'

'I'll have a word with David Porter before classes begin for the day,' Esther told her, then turned to Lily. 'Lily, dear, would you take Clarissa into class, please, then send David out here immediately?'

A nervous-looking David appeared at the front door minutes later, and Esther instructed him to follow her as she walked out of earshot of the pupils who were still arriving for the morning class. Turning to David, she asked, 'What's all this nonsense you've been telling Clarissa about a ghost in the basement?'

'It's not nonsense, honestly!' David insisted. 'It's the ghost of Lady Anne who's buried in the basement and who's waiting to steal a child from the school.'

'I'll give you full marks for your imagination, David,' Esther replied sternly, 'but I'd hoped for better from you than scaring your classmates with rubbish like that.'

'It's *not* rubbish!' David insisted. 'Mr Pilgrim told me all about what happened here in the past.'

'There are no such things as ghosts,' Esther said firmly, 'and I'll be having a few stern words with Mr Pilgrim. In the meantime, go back to your class, and let's hear no more nonsense about ghosts, or I'll put a black mark in your report for this term.'

David wandered sullenly back into the school, and as Pilgrim rang the bell for the start of classes, Esther asked him to stay back for a moment. 'Why have you been scaring the children with rubbish about the school being haunted by the ghost of Lady Anne?' she asked him.

'Beg pardon?'

'Don't try and claim innocence in the matter,' Esther insisted. 'I was told by David Porter that you'd been filling his head with some foolishness about the school basement being haunted.'

'I never said nowt of the sort,' Pilgrim replied indignantly.

'Are you calling David Porter a liar?'

'No, I'm just sayin' I never said nowt of the sort ter David Porter, an' if yer doesn't believe me then yer callin' *me* a liar, ain't yer?'

'Well, one of you is lying,' Esther insisted, 'but I'd rather that the entire business be dropped. There's no ghost in this school, and I don't want to hear any more suggestions that there is — from *anyone*, understood?'

'Yer still callin' me a liar, ain't yer?' Pilgrim grumbled. 'An' me an old soldier what were wounded in the service of 'er Majesty an' what's always been loyal ter this school, long afore *you* lot arrived 'ere.'

'A pity that your *loyal service* didn't include being able to fix those problems with the plumbing the other day,' Esther replied tartly, and Pilgrim's face reddened in anger.

'I weren't employed as a plumber, were I?' he retorted. ''T'ain't right, what you're saying, an' I'll be reportin' this conversation ter Miss Allsop, who I'm sure 'as an 'igher regard fer me services than *you* seem to 'ave. Is that all — can I go now?'

Emily was waiting for Esther as classes ended for the day. In a soft voice made hesitant by embarrassment she asked, 'Was it really necessary to upset Mr Pilgrim like that? He's made a formal complaint about what he called your "haughty manner". I'm sure you had your reasons, Esther, but just at the moment we're relying on him.'

'He was spreading rumours about the alleged ghost of Lady Anne,' Esther told her, 'and filling the children's heads with fear of attending school because there's a ghost in the basement. We surely don't need *that* at the moment, either.'

'That's a serious allegation, Esther, and I'd rather that you didn't antagonise Mr Pilgrim any further,' Emily insisted.

Esther pouted. 'Only two days ago we were asking ourselves whether Mr Pilgrim was quite up to the job, and whether his references might have been false. Did you instigate those enquiries you were planning to make?'

'No,' Emily admitted, 'chiefly because even if he *did* come with forged references, we can't afford to be without him at this sensitive time. So just try not to get his back up any more, if you'd be so good.'

Esther nodded without actually making any verbal promise, and collected Lily for the brief homeward walk. She was determined to unearth the truth of the matter, even if it wouldn't be to Emily Allsop's immediate liking.

CHAPTER FOUR

'I just can't imagine how he could have got all that background information,' Esther complained to a weary Jack over supper once the children had been fed and put to bed. 'Emily had to make enquiries of some local historical group, so how did Stanley Pilgrim learn about the story of the ghost? And it's not just that — there's the paint on the wall that the police didn't seem to want to take seriously, then there were those problems with the plumbing. Not only were they matters that any half-decent caretaker could have dealt with, but their causes were simple enough for a non-plumber to have brought about. And they happened on the very day that Emily was trying to persuade new parents that the school would be a suitable one for their offspring.'

'But why would a caretaker want to scupper his own school?' Jack asked. 'He'd be out of a job if he succeeded.'

Esther sighed. 'He had no reason of his own, clearly — but someone *else* had a motive for wanting to see the school fail.'

'Are you suggesting that someone put him up to it?' Jack asked. 'Someone bribed Pilgrim?'

'Yes … perhaps.'

'Well, if you want me to look into Pilgrim's background, I'll need his date of birth,' Jack told her.

Esther thought for a moment, then smiled. 'Emily has his references in her school records somewhere. I have access to those for my class registers, so I'll see if I can find out his birthday.'

'I'll also need the place where he was born,' said Jack.

'Do you want his hat size as well?'

'You're the one seeking my help,' Jack replied, 'and sarcasm doesn't suit you. Now, give me a kiss by way of my partial fee in advance.'

Jack cursed under his breath and screwed up his eyes in an attempt to clear the bleariness that came from reading one closely printed document after another.

Esther had so far produced nothing of any value in the search for whatever shady history her school caretaker might possess. Jack had no date of birth, no year of birth, and no place of birth, and although he'd been lucky in the sense that the name Stanley Pilgrim had not — as he had feared — resulted in a whole tribe of men with the same name when the Yard's criminal records had been consulted, this did not make his task any easier. All that Esther had been able to remember about Pilgrim was that he had claimed to be an old soldier wounded in the service of Queen Victoria.

The Second Boer War was still ongoing, so, considering that Pilgrim had been employed at the school for some years, he must therefore have been a casualty of the First Boer War. Jack had access to copies of all military service records, given the frequency with which men discharged from the army applied to join the Met, and so it was *simply* a matter of searching through all of them for a man named Stanley Pilgrim injured in combat.

He'd been at it for two days — time in which he ought really to have been processing recruit applications — and so far there was not a 'Pilgrim' in sight. He was about to call it a day when he caught the name 'Pilgrim' at the foot of a sheet dated February 1881. It recorded the terrible defeat inflicted on the British troops, consisting largely of one English infantry regiment and several drawn from the Scottish Highlands, at a place called Majuba Hill. The English infantry had been drawn from the Northamptonshire Regiment, and listed near the foot of the sad account of the casualties from that day was the following: *Lance Corporal Stanley Pilgrim, leg shattered by enemy artillery, died of his wounds in Volksrust Field Hospital, 3 March. Family in Shoreditch, London, informed by telegraph.*

This time the oath that escaped Jack's lips was audible two offices away. The only Stanley Pilgrim he could find who remotely resembled the one now employed as a caretaker at Cassiobury House School had died in South Africa almost ten years previously. The only thing that Jack could claim as a reward for two days of strained eyesight was the fact that there was a possible family connection in the East End. He switched to the enlistment rolls for the Northamptonshire Regiment, and discovered that there had been a recruitment officer from that regiment active in the Commercial Street area that acted as a boundary between Whitechapel and Shoreditch, to its north. This perhaps explained why, in 1877, a man called Stanley Pilgrim, with a home address in Hewett Street in Shoreditch, came to be an infantryman in a regiment based in a town seventy miles from his home.

Jack could take himself down to Shoreditch and make further enquiries, but he considered that he'd done more than enough already, and he had his own job to think about.

Back home that evening, Jack disclosed the outcome of his enquiries to Esther. 'Either your caretaker is a man with no criminal record, or he's someone pretending to be Stanley Pilgrim, for reasons that are not immediately obvious. Either way, your man is no wounded war veteran.'

'Then who is he?' Esther demanded.

'I have no idea,' Jack responded. 'You simply wanted to know if a man called Stanley Pilgrim had a criminal record, and the answer is no.'

'But we're no nearer to learning who he really is, and why he might have a grudge against the school,' Esther protested.

'We don't know that he does,' Jack reminded her, earning himself a snort of disbelief.

'Well, he's certainly been behaving as if he does, and for my money I'm going to assume that he's being paid by someone who *really* does.'

'Good luck with that,' Jack replied. 'You might wish to start by finding out if anyone had occasion in recent years to voice a grievance against the school. A disgruntled parent, an expelled pupil, someone along those lines. Or you might wish to ask whether or not Pilgrim has any other employers on the side. I would imagine that the wage paid to a school caretaker is not exactly large.'

'I think he does some work for the Earl of Essex sometimes,' Esther replied. 'Timber clearing, fencing, that sort of thing. He was at the fair, I noticed, helping with the ropes that cordoned off the performance area from the crowds. But why would the Earl of Essex want to subvert our school caretaker?'

'A question for you, clearly,' Jack reminded her. 'But don't forget that we've got the family arriving for Sunday lunch. We haven't seen Percy, Beattie, Lucy or Teddy once since we moved up here.'

Esther's suspicion that someone might be attempting to undermine Emily's attempts to revive the school was strengthened several days later when she arrived at the front gate to find Emily herding all the pupils into the yard, and advising them that they had been awarded an extra playtime.

Bemused by this change of routine, and given that the low scudding clouds suggested that rain was not far away, Esther walked over to Emily with eyebrows raised in a silent question.

'Come inside with me, but leave Lily to play with the others,' Emily instructed her hoarsely, then led the way into the Primary One classroom. Esther's mouth dropped open at what she saw. Written on the wall in what looked like the same red paint as before was the warning *Lady Anne wants a child — beware, all of you!*

'There's more of the same in my classroom,' Emily told Esther in a flat voice. Esther stepped across the hallway into Primary Two, where the message on the wall read *The ghost walks at midnight.*

'What does it mean?' Esther asked as she rejoined Emily in Primary One.

'I would have thought it obvious what it means,' Emily replied with a harsh laugh. 'More to the point, who did it? And how can we hold classes with — with *that* on the walls?'

'Have any of the children seen it yet?' Esther asked.

'No, and obviously I don't want them to. But what can we do with them until Mr Pilgrim's had time to remove it from both classrooms?'

'We can keep them outside,' Esther suggested, 'but it looks to be threatening rain out there, so a nature ramble is obviously out of the question. Get Mr Pilgrim started, and I'll organise some games on the grass area.'

Uncertain how long she could keep their attention, Esther sought inspiration as she walked back outside and whispered to Lily, 'What would your class most like to do for an hour or so?'

'Why can't we go into the classroom?' Lily asked unhelpfully.

'Mr Pilgrim has some urgent work to do in there. Now, how can we keep ourselves occupied in the meantime?'

'Has anyone asked us to perform our dance again, like the local church, or the people down at the soccer field?' Lily asked.

Esther let out a sigh of relief as she replied, 'Not yet, but they might if we practise it. Well thought of, Lily — you're really very inventive when you need to be.'

'I take after Papa, I think, or perhaps his Uncle Percy,' Lily said with a smile.

'I wouldn't want you becoming *that* inventive,' Esther replied, 'but let's see if we can remember the Chestnut Dance, shall we?'

The ruse was working well, and almost half an hour had passed when one of the Primary One girls — Charlotte Manners — uttered a piercing scream and pointed, wide-eyed, towards the shrubbery to one side of the lawn.

'The ghost!' she shouted as she took to her heels and ran back to the small yard in front of the school doors. Most of the rest of the group ran after her, yelling and screaming, leaving Esther, Lily and two of the boys staring intently into the trees and bushes, where there was clearly nothing to be seen. Just then, attracted by the noise, Emily appeared at the front doors and began enquiring of Charlotte what was going on. She then called to Esther, 'Mrs Enright, the children may resume their classes now.'

When Esther made no move to return to the school, Lily looked up at her enquiringly.

'Can we go back, Mama?'

'Not until I've proved once and for all that there's no ghost here,' Esther replied as she gritted her teeth and walked slowly towards the small copse.

'No, Mama — no!' Lily pleaded with her. 'Don't go in there — the ghost will get you!'

'Not if there isn't one,' Esther called back resolutely, though her heart pounded as she stepped forward. It was the work of only a few moments to satisfy herself that there was no sign of any ghost. She walked to the far edge of the copse and looked over the fence that marked the boundary of the Cassiobury House grounds. Behind the school was an open patch of rough ground between two of the houses that fronted Rickmansworth Road, giving a clear line of approach to anyone seeking to gain entry to the school grounds without going through its front entrance. Halfway down was a clump of trees that would make a convenient hiding place, but Esther had little difficulty in persuading herself that her ghost-hunting had gone far enough for one morning.

She was in the process of retracing her steps, her heartbeat returning to normal, when she noticed something light from the corner of her eye. The material was impaled on the thorns of a dog rose that had grown, presumably wild, between two chestnut saplings, and was a light grey in colour. Esther's previous livelihood as a seamstress and dressmaker enabled her to recognise the material as pompadour taffeta, and she knew two things about it. The first was that it was not cheap, and the second was that they had been making ladies' gowns from taffeta for centuries —probably as far back as the seventeenth century. If, as she suspected, someone had set out to simulate a ghost, then they had an eye for detail.

She rejoined a relieved-looking Lily on the grass, who asked, 'What's that in your hand?'

'Proof that the *ghost* is entirely earthbound,' Esther replied. She turned to the two boys who had remained with Lily. 'Time for classes, after all that exertion and excitement,' she told them all.

They were met at the front doors by Emily.

'Both classes are ready for their morning lessons, and thank you for holding the fort so brilliantly,' she told Esther.

'Did Mr Pilgrim manage to erase the writing?' Esther asked in a whisper.

'He didn't have time, so instead he painted right over it,' Emily whispered back.

'Using red paint?' Esther asked suspiciously.

'Yes — isn't he resourceful? You really do misjudge him, I think.'

'Well, ask yourself how he just happened to have a supply of *precisely* the same shade of paint,' Esther replied with knitted brows. 'Anyway, let's see what it looks like. I only hope that the children don't get headaches from the smell of all that paint.'

As she expected, there was a strong smell of paint in Primary One, but where there had once been an ominous warning there was now a strip of red paint running across the entire wall behind the blackboard. As a precaution, Esther asked Tommy Brailsford to open the three windows down the side of the room, in order to let in some fresh air.

By lunchtime they'd become used to the smell without any of the pupils complaining that they felt unwell. As they scuttled out of the classroom, some of them home to lunch, and the rest into the kitchen, where Mrs Finch, the cook, served them a suitably healthy meal, Emily appeared in the doorway to Primary One with a troubled look on her face.

'Esther, could you spare me a few moments, please?' she asked.

Esther put her cheese sandwich back into her bag as she nodded. 'Of course — what is it?'

'First of all, what happened out on the grass earlier this morning? And what were you carrying in your hand when you came back?'

'This,' Esther replied triumphantly as she opened her desk drawer and extracted the small piece of taffeta that she'd found impaled on the bush. 'I believe that it demonstrates beyond doubt that our so-called "ghost" — the one that Charlotte thought she saw — is very physical. It's called "taffeta" and people have been making dresses out of it for years. No doubt you have several of your own, although perhaps not in this shade of "ghost grey".'

'Please don't joke about it, Esther,' Emily replied as she sat down heavily on one of the school chairs, which fortunately was wide enough to accommodate the straight skirt of her charcoal-grey two-piece outfit. She looked Esther directly in the eye. 'I've seen the ghost myself,' she confessed. 'Last night.'

'You mean that you saw someone *dressed* as a ghost, trying to scare you out of your wits,' Esther replied.

'Well, they very nearly succeeded,' Emily muttered, then fell silent until Esther invited her to tell her about it.

'Well,' Emily began, 'it must have been in the early hours of the morning. I haven't enjoyed a good night's sleep recently, what with the worry of keeping the school going. Anyway, I distinctly heard what I can only describe as a thumping rattle on the window of my bedroom which, as you know, is on the first floor immediately above Primary Two, and looks out over the school grounds. I thought that perhaps a bird had flown into the window, but then of course I remembered the hour, and the unlikelihood that any birds would be flying at that time of night. Anyway, I looked out of the window and there was this figure — ghostly white, or perhaps light grey — gliding down the lawn where you took the children this morning.'

'You say "gliding"?' Esther asked. 'Not walking in a normal way?'

'No,' Emily replied 'Definitely gliding. It looked so eerie and bizarre, and I have to confess that it spooked me so much that I jumped back into bed and threw the covers over my head.'

'I'd probably have done the same,' Esther admitted, 'had I not found what I did today. Someone's clearly out to ruin this school, despite your efforts to revive it.'

'But why would anyone want to do that?' Emily asked. 'What have I ever done to deserve such treatment?'

'I don't know,' Esther replied in what she hoped was a friendly way. 'But now that I have something physical to show my doubting husband, it's about time that he lent a hand.'

'Mama chased a ghost today!' Lily told Jack gleefully as he was in the process of hanging his overcoat on the hall stand. 'She was ever so brave!'

'Really?' Jack asked with a raised eyebrow, looking at Esther as she stood in the hallway waiting for him. 'And did she get a name, address and place of birth this time?'

'No, I did not, but I did get *this*.' Esther produced the piece of taffeta. 'Physical proof that someone's trying to get the school closed down. There were more ominous warnings in red paint this morning, this time on the classroom walls. *And*,' she added for emphasis, 'Stanley Pilgrim has access to a supply of red paint.'

'Purely circumstantial,' Jack replied dismissively. 'What's for dinner?'

'Nothing, until you promise to investigate.'

'You want me to go hunting a ghost?' Jack asked with a quizzical grin.

Esther tutted. 'No — I want you to catch Stanley Pilgrim while he's up to his tricks.'

'His *alleged* tricks,' Jack corrected her.

'Very well, his *alleged* tricks,' Esther conceded. 'But last night he succeeded in playing the part of the ghost, and scared poor Emily half to death.'

'You're serious, aren't you?' Jack asked. 'All right, seeing as it's Saturday tomorrow, I'll go to the school with you and speak to Emily about what she thinks she saw. Will that be enough to qualify me for dinner?'

The following morning Emily shook Jack warmly by the hand. 'Thank you for taking the trouble to come and see what you can find out,' she said. 'Presumably Esther told you that I've seen the ghost for myself?'

'She did,' Jack replied. 'Tell me about your experience.'

Emily related the circumstances in which she'd come to see what she'd believed at the time to be the ghost of Lady Anne. Then, to the surprise of both ladies, Jack asked if the school possessed a stepladder. When a visibly grumpy Stanley Pilgrim was prevailed upon to produce it, Jack climbed up it outside Emily's window, gave the window frame a couple of firm shakes, then looked more intently at the glass itself. When he descended the ladder, it was with a knowing grin.

'You were deliberately roused from your bed to be shown the ghost,' he told Emily. 'The windowpane has become a bit loose in its frame, which is why it rattled when it was hit. As for the thump that you heard, it's still possible to see the mark left by the clod of earth that was thrown at it.'

'And Mr Pilgrim took the opportunity to recreate the ghost when I had the children on the grass next to the coppice,' Esther added eagerly.

Emily frowned. 'That can't be right, Esther,' she said, 'because at precisely that time he was painting over those dreadful messages on the classroom walls.'

'With the same red paint that he just happened to have in his possession!' Esther countered.

'Emily has a valid point, Esther,' Jack pointed out gently. 'Stanley Pilgrim can't have been in two places at once. So, either he must have had an accomplice, or he and another are both acting under the direction of a third person.'

'But whichever way you argue it,' Esther insisted, 'I'm right about Mr Pilgrim being involved, aren't I?'

'Almost certainly,' Jack agreed. 'But we don't know precisely how yet, or why.'

'And how do you propose to discover that?' Esther asked.

'I'll come back after dark and keep a look out,' Jack promised.

'And I'll keep watch from my bedroom window,' Emily said, to which Esther gave her grudging agreement.

CHAPTER FIVE

The local church clock chimed midnight as Jack stamped his feet as quietly as he could in order to restore the circulation to them. He stood under the eaves of the school's front doors, silently cursing his own impetuosity in agreeing to keep the premises under surveillance. He was reminded of lonely night beats in the mean alleyways of Whitechapel, and he'd rather not be. His attention was suddenly drawn to a movement on the far side of the lawn, in front of the copse of trees. Whatever it was appeared to be just over five feet tall, and it was gliding across the grass. Not walking — gliding. It was dressed in a long white or grey gown that reached down to the grass, and certainly looked very ghostly.

Jack stepped cautiously forward, keeping his eyes firmly fixed on the gliding form as it passed backwards and forwards across the lawn. He was within feet of it when he realised that even though the motion was a gliding one, it was audible as it rubbed across the coarse grass, and he thought he could just make out the sound of a woman breathing heavily with the effort of moving. Then there was a sharp blow to the back of his head and everything went dark.

Jack came round to be greeted by a throbbing sensation in his head and the sight of a man looming over him, armed with a club.

'Now then,' said the man, kneeling next to him on the grass, 'who are yer an' what yer doin' creepin' around these 'ere premises?'

'My name is Jack Enright, my wife is the deputy headmistress of this school, and I was investigating the possibility that the school has a ghost,' Jack replied groggily.

'Yeah, an' I'm the Queen o' Sheba,' the man replied sarcastically. 'Yer'll stay there 'til I calls the police.'

'Good luck with that,' Jack told him. 'I hear they are a waste of time around here. But at least I now know how the ghost was created.'

'What bleedin' ghost?' the man asked. 'I ain't seen no ghost, an' I'm the caretaker.'

'Well, I did,' came a voice from the front doorway. Emily Allsop appeared in her nightgown, a heavy coat over the top. 'From my bedroom window, just before you hit Mr Enright with that club in your hand. You had no right to do that, Mr Pilgrim.'

'I didn't 'it nobody,' Pilgrim protested, as Jack struggled to his feet.

'Well, *somebody* whacked me on the back of the head,' Jack complained as he reached up to feel where a bruise was already forming, 'and you're the one armed with what looks suspiciously like a billy club of the sort used by police officers.'

'I found this on the ground next ter yer,' Pilgrim insisted, 'but I didn't see no bloody ghost.'

'I'll perhaps report you for this,' Jack complained as he felt the lump again.

'Yer was trespassin', an' it's me job ter deal with trespassers,' Pilgrim replied indignantly. 'Anyroad, just be on yer way, an' we'll say no more about it.'

'I've already telephoned the police,' Emily told them, 'so perhaps you'd better both come inside and wait for them while I make some tea.'

Twenty minutes later, as Jack and Pilgrim sat glaring at each other, both armed with a mug of sweet tea and seated on chairs in the Primary Two classroom that were almost comically too small for them, Emily ushered Constable Jeffrey into the room.

'Now then,' the officer announced pompously as he extracted a notebook and pencil from the top pocket of his uniform jacket, 'I'm summoned here by this good lady to deal with a complaint that one man hit another over the head with a heavy wooden object. Which of you is the victim?'

'That would be me,' Jack confirmed, 'and you'll find the evidence of that in the form of a rapidly growing lump on the back of my head. But the gentleman responsible — *this* one —' he indicated with a nod towards Pilgrim — 'mistook me for an intruder.'

'I didn't 'it *nobody*!' Pilgrim insisted, and Jeffrey turned to address Emily.

'You summoned the police, Missus, so presumably you witnessed what transpired?'

'Yes,' said Emily, 'but I didn't actually see who administered the blow. Just a vague shadow that appeared from behind Mr Enright. He's the victim, as he says, and he was on the premises with my permission.'

'In the middle of the night?' Jeffrey asked disbelievingly. 'Might I ask for what purpose?'

'I was investigating the possibility that the school has a ghost,' Jack replied sheepishly, only too aware of how ridiculous that sounded.

'There ain't no ghost around 'ere,' Pilgrim insisted.

'Then what did I see gliding across the lawn?' Emily demanded, for which Pilgrim had no answer. At this point Jeffrey closed his notebook.

'I gather that you don't wish to press charges against this man,' he said to Jack while nodding towards Pilgrim. 'That being the case, I'll be on my way once you've given me some proof of your identity.'

'Is that really necessary, Constable?' Emily demanded. 'I already told you that his name's Enright. His wife is my deputy headmistress here at the school, and he was on the premises with my authority.'

Jeffrey's eyes narrowed. 'Are you the same Mr Enright who complained to my sergeant regarding the way I dealt with a complaint of criminal damage on these premises a couple of weeks ago? The same man who then wrote a snooty letter to our superintendent in Hertford regarding the pair of us?'

'Yes, that was me,' Jack conceded reluctantly.

'And from memory, you're high up in Scotland Yard, that right?'

'Also correct,' Jack confirmed. 'To be more precise, I'm Chief Inspector in charge of the Recruitment and Manpower division. And a word of advice, if I may, Constable Jeffreys — don't ever apply to transfer to the Met.'

Half an hour later, Jack let himself into the scullery to the rear of The Lodge. He'd chosen the trade entrance in the hope of not disturbing any of his sleeping family, but as he crept down the hall in stockinged feet, having abandoned his boots under the scullery sink, he saw a light under the sitting room door.

He opened the door quietly and saw Esther, curled up on the settee and wrapped in his old heavyweight police overcoat. Her eyes were closed, but as he turned away they opened, and she sat upright.

'How did it go?' she asked sleepily.

'I saw the ghost, then Pilgrim whacked me on the back of the head. You didn't need to wait up for me — it must be past one in the morning.'

'Did you really imagine that I would get any sleep, knowing that you were out there investigating in the school grounds? Are you hurt? Would you like me to make some tea?'

'I got a nasty bump to the head, but Miss Allsop made me some tea when she came downstairs after seeing me being attacked.'

'In her nightgown, no doubt?'

'Yes, but more to the point, she also saw the ghost. Pilgrim tried to deny seeing it, and even denied whacking me over the head. The local police officer was about as useful as a chocolate teapot.'

'Well, I'm going to make some tea, then I'll have a look at that bump to your head.'

'You can hardly miss it, but I'd rather just get some sleep.'

'If I can stay up to welcome you home, the least you can do is tell me all about the ghost,' Esther insisted as she brushed past him and walked towards the kitchen. 'Welcome back, by the way,' she added over her shoulder.

As they sat at the kitchen table, nursing mugs of hot, sweet tea, Jack recounted the events of the night.

Esther nodded. 'So, the ghost is definitely make-believe, is that what you're saying?'

'Without a doubt,' Jack confirmed. 'It was making a noise as its gown trailed across the grass, and I could hear a woman breathing heavily from the effort of "gliding" across it.'

'So, it is a woman?'

'You don't miss much, do you?' Jack said with a wink. 'More to the point, Pilgrim seemed determined not to let me any closer to it, although he denied being the one who whacked me across the bonce. Unfortunately, Miss Allsop didn't get a good look at who hit me, no doubt because she was too busy watching the ghost. By the time she got downstairs, it had gone.'

'Emily she saw the ghost as well?'

'She did,' Jack told her, 'although we didn't get around to discussing that in any great detail.'

'As she hastened to make you tea, while dressed in her nightgown?'

'I'm not sure what her nightgown has to do with all this, but yes, she made tea for both me and Pilgrim.'

'For Pilgrim? After he whacked you over the head?'

'He denied it, of course, but I'm certain it was him. Your suspicions against him have now become *my* suspicions against him. And of course, we can confirm, at least in our own minds, that the ghost is all part of a conspiracy to ruin the school.'

'Let's hope that it doesn't succeed,' Esther said as she suppressed a yawn. 'And perhaps we'd both better get some sleep, because the family will be here in pursuit of lunch before the day's much older.'

Jack woke the next morning to the alluring smell of a roast beef cooking, and he woke Esther with a gentle shake of the shoulder before wandering downstairs to order tea and muffins for two from Polly. He passed the open sitting room door, where Lily sat sewing something or other, while Bertie had a line of toy soldiers in battle formation, about to attack the sideboard. He looked up with a grin.

'Why have you got a big lump on the back of your head, and what time will the cousins be arriving?' he asked.

'Around noon, and is the lump on my head so obvious?' Jack asked. Bertie nodded, and Lily giggled.

'It looks like an Easter egg, Papa,' she told him.

Percy and Beattie were the first to arrive, a little after eleven-thirty. Jack walked ahead of them into the dining room, where Esther was waiting with the sherry decanter and a smile as she suppressed yet another yawn. As Percy fell into line behind Jack, he observed, 'Life in Recruitment and Manpower has obviously become more violent than is popularly believed. Or were you brutally chastised by Assistant Commissioner Bruce?'

'The source of my head extension will no doubt be the main topic of conversation over lunch,' Jack muttered, 'and if I fall asleep during the first course, put it down to my new career as a ghost-hunter.'

Jack stayed awake during the soup course, and was not even yawning when Polly entered proudly with the beef roast, while Alice laid the vegetable dishes down on the table. Jack carved the roast, and after he was warned by Aunt Beattie that if he placed one more slice of beef on Uncle Percy's plate he'd go to the bottom of her Christmas present list, everyone helped themselves to vegetables. It was silent apart from the eager clashing of cutlery, until Aunt Beattie observed laconically, 'I'm obviously destined to be the one to ask the question that's on everyone's mind. So tell us, Jack, how *did* you come by that massive lump on your head?'

'I was out ghost-hunting,' said Jack, 'when the ghost's minder took exception.'

It fell silent again as the guests considered whether the bump on Jack's head had resulted in brain damage. Esther stepped in.

'As usual, Jack's only telling part of the story. The school at which I teach has recently come under attack from someone determined to see it fold. It's a private school, as you may recall, and its proprietor is that lovely lady who I met at the teacher training college that I attended, and who invited me to become her Deputy Head. Anyway, for reasons that remain obscure, someone is trying to prevent her from building up the school's intake numbers from the low level they were at when she took over. It began with ominous messages daubed on the walls in red paint, then progressed into baseless rumours of a ghost stalking the grounds in search of a child to steal. Jack very gallantly offered to investigate the possibility that it was all a hoax, but just as he was about to make a very important discovery someone whacked him over the head. That was last night, and we apologise to you all if we've been yawning since you arrived, but neither of us enjoyed much sleep afterwards.'

'Getting whacked on the head was something I would have thought he'd got used to on the beat,' Percy observed. 'If we didn't get one of those at least once a week, we felt that we weren't doing our jobs properly.'

'So what serves as confirmation that you're doing things right, now that you're retired?' asked Teddy, who was married to Jack's sister Lucy.

'I wouldn't know,' Percy muttered, 'since I never do things right often enough for Beattie.'

'Perhaps you might wish to start by being home occasionally,' Beattie retorted bitterly. 'I think I saw more of you when you were working, and at least I knew what time you were *supposed* to be home. Since retiring,' she added, her eyes scanning everyone around the table, 'Percy leaves the house before breakfast, and is barely home in time for a late supper — when I consider that he deserves supper, of course. I assume that he eats out somewhere on those "long walks" that he claims to be taking.'

'At my age, one has to remain fit,' Percy replied, 'which includes going on long, invigorating walks and refraining from unhealthy eating habits.'

'Like five slices of beef?' Beattie asked pointedly, and Percy opted for a change of topic.

'Have you any idea who's behind this vendetta against the school, Esther?' Lucy asked.

'We suspect the school caretaker,' Esther replied, 'but as yet we haven't got enough evidence to confront him with our suspicions. Jack's convinced that he was the one who hit him over the head last night, and other circumstances suggest that he was behind certain earlier acts of vandalism, and the birth of ugly rumours that the school is haunted by the ghost of a woman who lived in a former house on the same spot several centuries ago. Cassiobury House can certainly be confirmed as the site of an old manor house during the Civil War days.'

'Talking of civil wars,' Jack put in, 'hadn't someone better check that the children haven't come to any harm in the park, or got themselves into any mischief?'

'I noticed the park on the way in,' Lucy said. 'It looks as if it might be the perfect location for open-air theatre. Does the local council own it?'

'No,' Esther told her, 'it's privately owned — the family estate of the Earl of Essex. We performed a dance there just a few weeks ago, at a fair to celebrate the formation of a new local soccer club. By we, I mean of course the children in the school I teach at, which hopefully will remain a school, despite whatever plans some secret adversary may have to prevent that.'

The following day, Monday, Emily was waiting by the front entrance to the school as the children were gathering ahead of the morning roll call. Sensing that Emily might wish to speak to her in confidence, Esther urged Lily to go over and speak with her friend Annabelle Pickering, who as usual was standing to one side of the happily chattering group, looking lost and despondent.

Safe from being overheard, Emily asked after Jack's health. 'I'm *so* sorry that he was hit over the head like that. Is he fully recovered?'

'Apart from the embarrassment of looking as if he's growing a coconut on the back of his head, yes, he is,' Esther said with a grin. 'As usual, Jack's pride takes longer to heal, and the children have proved merciless in constantly referring to his "extra head". It was a pity that you didn't actually see who did it, but he's convinced that it was Mr Pilgrim.'

'It almost certainly was,' Emily confided, 'but I couldn't honestly say that I saw him clearly. There was just a shadow armed with a club of some sort, and by the time that I got down there, Mr Pilgrim was claiming that he found the club lying next to Jack. He insisted that he thought he was dealing with an intruder.'

'But surely, if he did believe that, then he had nothing to lose by admitting to being the one who struck the blow?' said Esther.

Emily shrugged. 'You'd think so. However, if it makes you feel any better, I'm now a little suspicious of him myself. For one thing, Jack was making no noise as he crept up on the ghost, so how could Mr Pilgrim claim to have been alerted to his presence?'

'A good point. But since you've just mentioned it, Jack says that you claimed to have seen the ghost as well?'

Emily nodded. 'Yes, just like last time, gliding across the lawn. I was keeping watch from my bedroom window while Jack was creeping towards it. That's when he got hit from behind. But Mr Pilgrim claims not to have seen any ghost —

so you can perhaps understand why I was somewhat confused when I called the police.'

'Jack says that the constable who called was the same one who came to investigate that first outbreak of graffiti,' Esther said, 'and that he was as useless this time as on the previous occasion.'

'To be fair to Constable Jeffreys, even Jack conceded that he might have been mistaken for an intruder. But that only makes sense if Mr Pilgrim had been the one to hit Jack, whereas he claims that he wasn't. The constable didn't seem to think it appropriate to challenge him on that point, which I thought was rather inefficient of him. He seemed more interested in learning Jack's identity, and I was able to assure him that Jack had authority to be here, even at that late hour. Anyway, Jack's recovered, so that's all to the good, and no harm done.'

'Jack is convinced that the so-called ghost is nothing of the sort, and that it was a woman dressed up to look like a ghost?'

Emily's eyebrows rose in surprise. 'Really? Well, I hope you don't think it was me.'

'No, not for a moment. From what Jack told me, you appeared from inside the school, in your nightgown, just as he was picking himself up off the ground.'

'Yes, that's right. I barely had time to throw my coat on and slide into my boots, then run down the stairs to telephone the police. Anyway, here comes Mr Pilgrim with the class bell, so perhaps you'd be so good as to supervise the lines and the walk inside to classes.'

CHAPTER SIX

The following day Emily again sought out Esther as she sat at her desk eating her cheese sandwich. Esther could see from her expression that something was troubling her.

'I won't beat about the bush, Esther,' she began. 'I've had an anonymous letter. It claims to be from a concerned parent, and although no name was supplied, the handwriting looks vaguely familiar. An educated hand, anyway. Regrettably, it accuses me of — well, of immoral behaviour. With your husband.'

Esther wasn't sure whether to laugh or not. Then she remembered that the two had been in each other's company while Emily was clad in only a nightgown, and that Jack had not returned home until at least one o'clock on Sunday morning. She waited for Emily to continue.

'The allegation is completely false. I wouldn't — I *couldn't*… Please believe me, Esther, when I say that it would never even occur to me, and given that Jack had just been whacked on the head — well, I can assure you…' Emily's voice trailed off.

Esther took pity on her, and switched topics slightly. 'If you say that the letter was anonymous, how can you be sure that it was from a parent?'

'I can't, obviously, and I can only hope that it wasn't, because it went on to threaten to remove their "precious child" from the school, and to assure me that the "dreadful moral transgression" of which I'd been guilty would be revealed to other parents.'

'Did it mention Jack by name?'

'There was no mention of Jack, you'll be relieved to learn, but it did refer to the "scandalous goings-on" late on Saturday evening. So it must be someone who has been alerted to the fact that there was a man on the premises then.'

'And who else knew about that, apart from you and Jack and the police constable?' Esther challenged.

'Mr Pilgrim, you mean?'

'Who else? He may even have written the letter.'

'Out of the question,' Emily insisted. 'The man is all but illiterate, whereas the hand that wrote that letter was well educated. As I mentioned, I think I've seen it before, but I can't quite place where or when. Perhaps I've received a letter from the same parent in the past.'

'Well, we'll just have to hope that it *wasn't* a parent, or, if it was, that they don't carry out their threat. We've just begun to turn the corner on enrolment numbers, and we can't afford a setback like this right now.'

Her words seemed almost prophetic when, the following day, the worst setback of all occurred.

Wednesday began like every other school day, with the morning roll call at eight-thirty and lessons from nine until noon. During the lunch break, while those who went home for their midday meal left the premises, the majority of the pupils enjoyed a healthy meal prepared by Mrs Finch in her kitchen. They ate in a little room that had once been a scullery in the days when the house had been privately owned. Once they had eaten, they were free to play in the school grounds until Pilgrim rang the one-thirty bell. Then they formed up in lines in front of the front doors, ready to walk in an orderly fashion back into their classrooms for the afternoon roll call.

The afternoon roll call revealed that Annabelle Pickering was missing.

Esther assumed that she would, as pupils often did, rush in at the last minute with an apology.

When she did not, Esther asked of the class, 'Has anyone seen Annabelle since lunchtime?' Since Annabelle was one of those who took her midday meal on the school premises, it was likely that one of the pupils would remember seeing her. Lily raised her hand. Esther nodded at her to speak.

'I saw her while I was playing at skipping with Caroline. She was watching us.'

'That's right,' Caroline Edgerton confirmed. 'I invited her to join in, but she didn't answer. She was standing in front of the bushes and trees on the far side of the lawn.'

'Perhaps she didn't hear the bell and has lost track of the time,' Esther suggested. She asked Lily to go outside and look for her.

Lily returned, shaking her head. 'I looked everywhere,' she said breathlessly, 'even in the lavatories, but she's nowhere to be seen.'

Leaving the pupils with an exercise to complete in their jotters, Esther crossed the hallway and knocked on the door to Primary Two. When Emily came to the door, Esther whispered, 'Annabelle Pickering is missing. She wasn't at afternoon roll call and was last seen by the copse on the far side of the lawn. Where you and Jack saw the ghost,' she added as an unwelcome afterthought.

Emily's face paled as she asked Esther to return to Primary One while she instructed Pilgrim to search the house and grounds for the missing girl.

'Can he be trusted?' Esther asked.

'Do you have a better suggestion?' Emily replied.

Conceding that she didn't, Esther returned to her class and occupied them for the remainder of the afternoon in some difficult arithmetic exercises that she hoped would take their minds off the fact that one of their classmates had disappeared. When four o'clock came, and the pupils headed home in their customary noisy fashion, Esther crossed the hallway and anxiously asked Emily whether Pilgrim had found Annabelle.

'No,' Emily replied, her face even paler than it had been earlier. 'She must have left the school premises at lunchtime, so she could be anywhere.'

'If someone is playing cruel games in an attempt to close the school down, then could it be that they have snatched Annabelle?' Esther suggested.

'That doesn't bear thinking about, Esther,' Emily replied, her voice cracking with emotion. 'There must be another explanation.'

'Well, Annabelle can be a bit absent-minded. I wouldn't put it past her just to have wandered off. Perhaps she's even taken herself home without telling us. We'd look foolish if we claimed that she'd gone missing, only to find that she was sitting at home all along.'

Emily nodded. 'I think her father only placed her with us in the hope that she'd make friends and become more — well, sociable, I think.'

'She has one friend at least,' Esther suddenly remembered. 'Lily felt a little sorry for her when she didn't seem to have any friends, and befriended her. Perhaps she can shed some light on where Annabelle might have gone. She's waiting for me in the classroom — shall we ask her?'

'Of course,' Emily agreed. 'We've got nothing to lose at this stage.'

Lily was invited into the Primary Two classroom. 'Lily, Annabelle is still missing and we need your help to find her,'

Esther said. 'Could she have simply gone home without telling anyone?'

'I don't think so,' Lily said. 'She's not happy at home, so I don't think she'd have gone back there.'

'Why isn't she happy at home?' Esther asked.

'It's her stepfather. Her real father died, and her mother married again when Annabelle was just little, and her new father's very strict. Annabelle believes that she's not good enough, which is why she's so shy and can't make friends. It took simply *ages* before she told me how unhappy she is at home, and I'm supposed to be her friend. It wouldn't surprise me if she's run away from home. When can *we* go home, Mama?'

'I have a few things I need to discuss with Miss Allsop before we can leave,' Esther told her daughter. 'I promise I'll be as quick as I can.'

Lily departed with a sullen pout, and Esther turned back to Emily. 'If Annabelle *has* run away from home, how can we tell her parents?'

'We don't know that she has run away,' Emily reminded her, 'but if we don't tell Mr and Mrs Pickering that Annabelle wasn't in school this afternoon, it can only make matters worse. It is my responsibility as headteacher to let them know that she's missing.'

'You're right,' Esther agreed, 'but I don't envy you the task. Would you like me to come with you?'

'No, thank you,' Emily said with a small smile. 'It's more appropriate coming from me. You take Lily home.'

Back at home, Esther was so preoccupied with the latest misfortune to befall the school that she could barely give sensible instructions to Polly regarding the evening meal. Jack saw the look on his wife's face as soon as he returned from work. 'Bad day at school?' he asked.

Esther nodded distractedly. 'One of the girls has gone missing.'

'When you say *missing* —' Jack began, but Esther cut him off.

'She was last seen on the grass at lunchtime, by that line of trees and shrubs where you saw the ghost on Saturday night. Then she didn't answer the afternoon roll-call. We don't know if she's just wandered off home, or been abducted, or … well, we just don't know. And I had to leave it to Emily to let her parents know.'

'Have you informed the police?'

'How could we, when for all we know she just went wandering? And in any case, you know as well as I do how useless the local constable is.'

'Even so…' Jack began.

'Why don't *you* go looking for her?' Esther demanded angrily.

'I don't know what she looks like, for one thing,' he objected.

'Well, Lily does, because she's her friend. You could take her with you.'

'It might be better to wait and see if there's a ransom note,' Jack suggested. When Esther returned a blank look, he added, 'Well, if she *has* been abducted, you'd have to hope that it was for the purposes of ransom, in which case there'll be a note.'

'And if she has been abducted and there's *no* ransom note?'

'We just have to hope there is, that's all,' he replied with a grave expression.

CHAPTER SEVEN

After a sleepless night, Esther was met by Emily at the front doors of the school the following morning.

'I've received a note demanding five thousand pounds for Annabelle's return,' Emily told her.

They hurried indoors, and Esther took a seat in Primary Two as Emily fumbled in her bag and produced the note in question.

'It was pushed under the front doors sometime during the night — I found it when I was going out for my morning walk,' Emily explained. 'Needless to say, I didn't proceed with my intended walk after I'd opened the note and read it.'

Emily handed Esther the note. It had been compiled from words that had obviously been cut from a local newspaper, then pasted onto a single sheet of paper. It read:

Five thousand pounds to be left under the large oak at the edge of the trees on your side of the fence if you want the girl back alive. You will be told when. No police or she dies.

'Jack said there might be a note,' Esther told Emily. 'At least we know that Annabelle is still alive.'

'If you can believe what the note says,' Emily grimaced. 'It could be a cruel hoax.'

'We have to proceed on the basis that it isn't,' Esther insisted. 'But whoever wrote it clearly knows the layout of the school premises, which again suggests Mr Pilgrim's involvement in some way. And the reference to "your side" suggests that whoever it is will approach from that vacant land on the other side of the fence behind the trees.'

'Let's hope that they keep their side of the bargain when the time comes,' Emily said, 'and deliver Annabelle back safely.'

'Forgive me for asking, Emily,' said Esther, 'but can you lay your hands on five thousand pounds?'

'Of course I can, given the value of the school and its grounds. The bank will presumably accept those in security of a loan.'

'And what about not involving the police?'

Emily answered with a wry smile. 'Funnily enough, that was Mr Pickering's wish as well.'

'I'm sorry, I forgot to ask,' Esther apologised. 'How did he take the news of Annabelle's disappearance?'

'He was strangely stoic about it, although predictably he was very critical of the school's lack of supervision. However, it was his opinion that if we involved the police this might precipitate panic on the part of whoever might be holding Annabelle. That was curious as well — he seemed to assume that Annabelle had been kidnapped, and of course I didn't have the note then. He was most businesslike in his attitude, but Mrs Pickering more than made up for that in tears. She was very upset, as you might expect.'

'So if you're not going to involve the police, will you simply hand over the money?'

'I certainly won't inform the police of what's happened, given that they appear to be about as reliable as wet paper, but I am considering another possible course of action that I won't disclose at present. I've already telephoned someone who might be able to help. I'll keep you advised on what steps we're going to take. In the meantime, classes as usual.'

'Classes as usual' proved to be an optimistic forecast. For one thing, a general air of gloom seemed to have descended on Primary One, and two of the children were missing. It would later be revealed, by way of notes sent to Emily, that their parents had temporarily withdrawn them, given that the school had inexplicably allowed a pupil to vanish when she should have been carefully and closely supervised. It now seemed as if the remaining pupils had somehow picked up the feeling that Cassiobury House was no longer a safe place to be.

Midway through the morning Esther abandoned her attempt to engage her pupils in basic geometry. After rubbing out the image of an isosceles triangle from where she'd drawn it on the board, she asked, 'Well, class, what *do* you all want to do this morning?'

It fell silent, until eventually Caroline Edgerton asked, 'Is it true that the ghost of the Grey Lady took Annabelle?'

'What on earth made you ask that?' Esther asked, aghast.

'It's what everyone's saying,' Caroline replied by way of justification.

'And who's *everyone*?' Esther demanded.

'Well, Mr Pilgrim,' Caroline replied.

Esther was sorely tempted to disclose that the same Mr Pilgrim had emphatically denied the existence of any ghost late on Saturday night, after whacking her husband over the head with a billy club, but instead she sought clarification.

'When did Mr Pilgrim say that, and to whom exactly did he say it?'

'He said it to all of us, Mrs Enright,' Tommy Brailsford chimed in. 'We were a bit slow getting into our lines, and Mr Pilgrim said, "Look snappy about it, or the ghost'll get you like it got Annabelle."'

'Let me assure you all,' said Esther loudly, looking around the class, 'that Cassiobury House has no ghost, and that whatever has happened to Annabelle — wherever she's got to — she was *not* taken by a ghost.'

The expressions on the faces of the pupils reflected their lack of conviction, so Esther tried another approach.

'Can any of you tell me what a ghost actually is?'

'It's somebody who's died,' Tommy replied confidently.

'And what happens to people's bodies when they die?' Esther asked.

There was a brief silence before Caroline spoke. 'When my grandmama died, they put her in a box in the ground.'

'Exactly,' Esther confirmed. 'So, how could they possibly be able to get out and walk around?'

There was no response to this, so Esther decided to quit whilst she was ahead.

'The so-called Grey Lady has been in her box for over three hundred years, hasn't she? So let's not hear any more silly stories about ghosts — from *any* of you. Now, let's see how good you are at remembering what we talked about yesterday — there will be class points for those of you who can recall who Julius Caesar was.'

The morning passed without any further reference to ghosts, but when lunch was over, and the pupils went out to play, it was noticeable that they confined their games to the hard area in front of the school doors, and that none of them ventured onto the grass. Esther had just finished her sandwich when Emily appeared in her doorway.

'Esther, do you have a moment? I'd like you to meet someone who will hopefully be able to discover what's being going on around here recently, and who can advise us on how to respond to the kidnapper's demands. He's an enquiry agent up from London, and he comes highly recommended by the Managing Director of Debenhams in Wigmore Street. Here's his business card — he's upstairs having tea in my sitting room if you'd care to go up.'

Esther rose from her desk and walked into the hallway. As she took the stairs up to Emily's private apartment, she glanced down at the business card. It read: *Percival Enquiry Agency. Confidentiality guaranteed. Twenty-four hour service, seven days a week. No assignment too difficult.*

There followed a telephone number and an address in Devonshire Road, Hackney. Esther was just reflecting on the fact that she had relatives in Hackney, when she reached the sitting room door. It was wide open, and Esther saw a man seated in Emily's best armchair, drinking tea.

It hardly came as a shock.

'Hello, Uncle Percy.' She gave him a warm smile.

'Quite like old times,' Percy said with a grin as Esther took the chair opposite his. 'Enrights combining to solve mysteries, and once again Esther is at the heart of the investigation.'

'Hopefully this one won't place my life in danger — or Jack's, for that matter,' she replied. 'But what on earth made you decide to become an enquiry agent?'

'Boredom, principally,' Percy explained. 'You'll no doubt find that Jack suffers from the same complaint when he finally retires. Once you get the investigating bug there's no cure for it, and you find yourself looking at seemingly innocent events with a cynical eye, even in retirement. Why did that woman next door wait until ten-thirty to take the milk from the front steps, when she normally does it before her husband leaves for work? Why did that man cross the road when he saw the local vicar approaching him? It's a habit that just won't go away.'

'Obviously not, in your case, but what does Aunt Beattie have to say about you opening up your own detective agency?'

'I prefer the term enquiry agent, but the answer to your question is that she didn't know until three hours ago. I had to tell her because I don't expect I'll be able to get home this evening. The train service into central London from Hackney is all but non-existent, and the horse bus takes forever, so if I'm to conduct any meaningful business here I'll need to impose upon your hospitality.'

'It goes without saying that you can stay with us for as long as you need to,' Esther said reassuringly. 'But what was Aunt Beattie's reaction?'

'Frosty, as you can imagine,' Percy replied with one of his impish grins. 'But I think she was only too relieved to learn that my lengthy absences from home every day were not in order that I might pursue a liaison with another woman. I can't help it if my debonair and dashing good looks render that an ongoing possibility.'

Esther chuckled. 'Your capacity for self-delusion clearly didn't retire when you did. Do you have a legitimate office, with staff, or are you operating from home? According to your business card you appear to have a business address in Devonshire Road, but I know that your house is in Victoria Park Road.'

'Indeed. Devonshire Road is a leisurely ten-minute stroll away, where I have two rooms above a candle shop, and a very efficient assistant who mans the telephone and deals with personal callers when I'm elsewhere, engaged in enquiries. He's a former police constable called Rufus Tomkins, invalided out on a pension when his leg was shattered by a bunch of drug importers in the London Docks.'

'And how many enquiries have you succeeded in conducting?'

'Enough to pay Rufus's weekly wage and, more recently, to keep the tobacco in my pipe. Most of the work has involved following errant husbands at the behest of suspicious wives, but this latest case promises to be of a higher standard, and it'll add to my portfolio of successful engagements.'

'So, did the Managing Director of Debenhams stray from the marital straight and narrow, or did that testimonial come from your fertile imagination?'

'No, the recommendation is genuine enough, but I'll keep that story until I can relate it to Jack at the same time, since it ties in with matters that have recently been causing the Yard some concern. More to the point, you are supposed to be providing me with more background on the matter that's brought me here.'

'One more question, if I may,' Esther said. 'How did you learn of the need for your services here at Cassiobury House School?'

'From you, of course,' Percy replied with a grin. 'During that excellent recent lunch at your house, you told us all about it. It was then a simple matter of sending a copy of my business card to your employer, the delightful Miss Allsop, along with a copy of the reference from Debenhams, the department store of choice for all fashionable ladies. Now, from what I can gather, there have been certain incidents of an annoying nature, followed by the recent disappearance of one of your school pupils, am I correct?'

'You are, but I obviously don't know how much Emily — Miss Allsop — has already told you.'

'Regardless, I'd like to hear your version anyway.'

'Well,' Esther began, 'it started with some graffiti on the front wall.'

'I gather that your graffiti was not of the obscene variety, and may even have been spelled correctly?'

'True. The graffiti made reference to the alleged presence within the school grounds of the ghost of a woman called Lady Anne, who is alleged to be searching for a long-lost child. Lost during the Civil War, as it happens. Then it escalated into threats that the ghost would take one of our pupils as a substitute. As you will appreciate, the fact that one of our pupils disappeared a few days ago has led to wild speculation that the ghost — popularly known as the Grey Lady — was responsible. We believe that the entire business is a plot to bring down the school, which was in a rundown state with very few pupils when Emily took it over, and is now under threat of losing more.'

'So some sort of attack on the business of the school?'

'Yes, or so we believe. And whoever is behind it has gone to considerable trouble, even to the point of manufacturing the ghost in question. Emily's seen it twice, and Jack encountered it last Saturday night. He was keeping watch in the school grounds when someone whacked him on the back of the head. Incidentally, you can still see the lump. He's very sensitive about it, so when you meet up with him over dinner you might want to keep the funnies to a minimum.'

'And who does Jack suspect of whacking him across the head?'

'The same man we suspect of being behind all of this — the school caretaker. He calls himself Stanley Pilgrim, except Jack found out that Stanley Pilgrim died almost twenty years ago.'

'Perhaps it is just a coincidence — there is bound to be more than one man with the name Stanley Pilgrim,' Percy suggested.

Esther shook her head vigorously. 'This Stanley Pilgrim claims to have acquired an injured leg during the previous Boer War, and by a strange coincidence a man of that name acquired just such an injury, except in his case it proved fatal. Also, it was Mr Pilgrim who first started spreading rumours of the ghost, which he later denied having done, *and* he had access to the same red paint that was used to create the messages on the walls. Then there were crude attempts to interfere with the school plumbing that Mr Pilgrim could easily have caused. He later claimed the problems were beyond his capacity to fix, although a local plumber dealt with them in less than an hour. Jack suspects that Mr Pilgrim was the one who whacked him on the head because when he came round, Mr Pilgrim was standing over him with a billy club. Of course, he denies that as well.

'It rather sounds as if I should begin by interviewing Mr Pilgrim,' Percy suggested, to an enthusiastic nod from Esther.

'I agree, although Emily seems rather reluctant to suspect him.'

'And indeed,' Percy observed, 'one would have to ask why a school caretaker would be taking steps to ruin the business that employs him.'

'Jack thinks that there are others behind it, and that Mr Pilgrim is simply being paid to do the dirty work, since he conveniently lives on the school premises. Anyway, I have to leave you now, Percy, to prepare for the afternoon class. No doubt Emily can arrange for you to interview Mr Pilgrim. If you join me outside the school gates at around four o'clock this afternoon, you can walk Lily and myself back to the house.'

CHAPTER EIGHT

'I don't know owt about that,' Pilgrim insisted when Percy asked him about the graffiti on the school walls. Percy was seated on a rickety old chair, while Pilgrim was seated on the side of a bed jammed against the wall, the sheets of which looked like they hadn't been washed since their purchase. The only other furniture in the cramped hut that passed for the caretaker's living quarters was an old stove, on top of which sat a pan that was inches deep in congealed fat.

'Yet you appear to possess a supply of precisely the same colour paint,' Percy reminded him as he nodded towards a tin in a corner of the hut. 'That was how you were able to erase the second round of wall daubing, was it not? If you had the paint available, why didn't you do the same thing with the first lot of graffiti, on the front wall above the school entrance?'

'Miss Allsop said ter scrape if off,' Pilgrim replied, 'an' so I did, usin' turpentine an' a scrubbin' brush.'

'To achieve that, you were obviously required to climb a ladder,' Percy observed. 'You managed that, despite your war wound?'

'Yeah, well, that were one of me better days,' Pilgrim growled.

'Talking of your wound, how exactly did you come by it?'

'At Majuba 'ill, it were,' Pilgrim replied. 'A bloody great cannon shot got me leg.'

'Left or right?'

'Pardon?'

'Left leg or right leg?' Percy asked by way of clarification.

'Left,' Pilgrim replied after a moment's hesitation.

'Which regiment were you in?'

'The Northamptonshire lot,' Pilgrim replied. 'There was lots o' them Scotch men there an' all.'

'A Londoner in a Northamptonshire regiment?' Percy queried. 'You *are* a Londoner by birth, I assume, from your accent?'

'Yeah — Shoreditch.'

'Which street in Shoreditch?'

'Hewett Street. Why?'

'And your injury will be listed in regimental records?'

'I dunno. They give a pension, anyroad, so that should be in their records.'

'Why did you tell the children about a ghost haunting the school and its grounds?'

'I just said that ter scare the kids — annoyin' little buggers, that they are,' he grunted.

'So you don't believe that the school has a ghost?'

'Course I bleedin' don't — I've never seen one, an' what I can't see I don't believe in.'

'I'm told that the ghost has in fact been seen twice by Miss Allsop, and once by a man who was patrolling the grounds at Miss Allsop's request, late last Saturday night. A man you hit on the back of the head with something heavy and blunt, like that old police club that I can see sticking out from under the bed.'

Pilgrim fell for that simple ruse, his eyes hastily turning to the bed as his face registered alarm. He looked back at Percy with a snarl.

'That were a cheap trick — there's no club under the bed.'

'Perhaps you've forgotten where you hid it after you hit the man on the head,' Percy suggested, deliberately not referring to

Jack by name, and hoping that Pilgrim wasn't making any connection between the two Enright men.

'I didn't 'it *nobody* on the 'ead,' Pilgrim insisted. 'An' as far as I knew, the man were a trespasser. Miss Allsop didn't warn me about someone bein' given permission ter creep around the place late at night.'

'So how did you know that he was?' Percy asked.

'I 'eard 'im, didn't I?'

'Even though your hut's a good few yards away from where you struck him? You must have very good hearing, if he was creeping around, as you said.'

'I *didn't* 'it 'im,' Pilgrim snarled. 'I already told yer.'

'So you went in search of an intruder unarmed?' Percy asked sceptically. 'And if he *was* an intruder, as you genuinely believed, then you'd have been entitled to hit him, wouldn't you?'

'Maybe — but I *didn't*!' Pilgrim all but shouted. 'What's this about, anyroad? I've got duties ter see to.'

'That's all right, Mr Pilgrim,' Percy reassured him. 'I've learned all I needed to know, and thank you for your time. I'll leave you to remember where you hid that club.'

'He was lying through his stained teeth,' Percy said as they sat around the dinner table later that evening. Jack had overcome his surprise at finding Percy waiting for him when he got home, and was now nodding as Percy confirmed the opinion that both he and Esther had formed regarding Pilgrim's involvement in whatever was going on at the school.

'But do you believe he is behind this apparent plot to ruin the school, or is he just the henchman?' Jack asked.

Percy snorted. 'It would be difficult to find anyone with *less* intelligence, so the answer to your question is yes, there is someone else involved. But that doesn't take us much further, does it?'

'So what's your next step?' Jack asked.

'I think I'll probe further into his background, in the hope of making some connection with a possible enemy of the school,' Percy replied, 'although it seems unlikely that a lowlife from the depths of Shoreditch would have a prior connection with a private school in Watford.'

'I took that as far as I was able,' Jack told him, 'and there's no doubt that Stanley Pilgrim died out in South Africa. But I didn't have time to go looking for someone who might be posing as him.'

'Did you consult the census records?' Percy asked.

'No, why?'

'They would have supplied all the information you required on other family members, assuming that they all lived in the same house. I'm surprised that an officer as senior as yourself didn't take such an obvious next step.'

Sensing the cooling atmosphere between uncle and nephew, Esther quickly diverted the conversation. 'You promised to tell me about the Managing Director of Debenhams, Percy, and how he came to give you a testimonial.'

'Ah, yes,' said Percy. 'You may find this of interest, Jack, given the problems the Met are currently facing.'

'What problems would they be?' Jack asked disingenuously.

'Don't give me that,' Percy retorted. 'Every officer in the Met, and a few thousand people outside it, are well aware that gangs of Russian immigrants are running the local force ragged, particularly in the East End.'

'Even if they are,' Jack countered, 'what have these gangs got to do with department stores like Debenhams?'

'Everything, as it transpires,' Percy assured him. 'While the menfolk are running what our American cousins call protection rackets among local shopkeepers — particularly among the Jewish community, many of whom are immigrants and therefore more vulnerable — their wives and mistresses are visiting department stores and stealing whatever takes their fancy. They dress as ladies of breeding and wealth, saunter around the clothing racks and lift items up, as if admiring them with a view to purchase. Then their accomplices gather round them in a huddle, blocking them from the view of the salespeople, and they slip the item under their voluminous clothing. It's even easier if the items are smaller, like jewellery, handbags and fans, in which case they just get slipped into a pocket. It's costs the department stores thousands a year in losses. But I'm delighted to report that thanks to me they're giving Debenhams a wide berth.'

'Why is that?' asked Jack as he helped himself to more potatoes, before Percy accounted for them all.

'What do you think is the greatest deterrent to committing crime?' Percy asked.

'The likelihood of a long prison sentence?' Esther suggested.

'That's what most people think. But in fact the greatest deterrent is the prospect of getting caught. When contemplating a crime, if you were guaranteed to get caught and punished, would you still commit that crime?'

'I wouldn't anyway,' Esther replied, 'if only because my conscience wouldn't let me.'

'You're presupposing the existence of a conscience,' Percy said. 'If you don't have one in the first place, then the only deterrent is a guarantee of getting caught. There goes your good name, your position in society, and your freedom for however many years the magistrate or judge sends you away.

We no longer deport people to Australia, but anyone who's spent even an hour in Newgate or Pentonville will confirm that it's not a desirable residence. In fact, it's to be avoided at all costs. So, make potential thieves believe that they *will* get caught, and they won't steal.'

'An admirable theory,' Jack observed, 'but almost impossible to achieve in practice. You can't have constables on duty alongside every counter or clothing rack in every department store.'

'Of course you can't,' Percy conceded, 'and that's why my strategy for Debenhams was so acceptable to them, and so effective against pilfering.'

It fell silent as Jack and Esther waited for Percy to explain.

'I came up with the idea that Debenhams should employ their *own* police. Not uniform constables, obviously, but individuals posing as ordinary shoppers — male and female — who collared anyone they saw attempting to steal an item. I gave them a very brief education in how to spot a thief and then set them to work.'

'And did it prove effective?' Esther asked.

Percy nodded. 'Of course it did, hence my testimonial from the Managing Director. No-one steals from his department store anymore because the would-be thieves find it much easier, and certainly less hazardous, to steal from rival stores.'

'How long did it take for the thieves to realise that there were what you might call "private store detectives" operating inside Debenhams?' Jack asked. 'The word would not have got out until a few collars had been felt, obviously.'

'I involved another member of the Enright family for that,' Percy said, chuckling. 'We decided to stage a few *pretend* apprehensions, and members of Lucy's theatre group proved most willing, and most effective. One of the actors posed as a thief caught in the act, while another made a very loud and public display of collaring them and hauling them off to the manager's office to await the police. Nothing can be more off-putting for a potential thief than the sight and sound of a wailing woman being hauled off for a spell in the chokey.'

'So Lucy knows all about your new business enterprise?' Esther asked.

Percy shook his head. 'Not the full extent of it — I just said that I was acting as a security consultant to Debenhams, which, of course, I was.'

'I don't suppose that the gangs currently running the East End have any such fear of getting caught,' Jack observed gloomily. 'They seem to be acting with impunity.'

'But the same psychology may be applied, even against them,' Percy suggested. 'Find out what they most fear, and somehow suggest that it will come to pass if they continue to break the law. In the case of these Russian immigrants — who in the main are fleeing from persecution back in their homeland — that greatest fear is likely to be being sent back.'

'That was certainly my parents' greatest fear,' Esther admitted. 'They came originally from Lithuania and were perfectly law-abiding, of course, but they feared that we would be thrown out of Spitalfields because there were too many immigrants living there. In addition, we were accused of having stolen the garment trade from those who were there before us. So yes, if you had wanted my parents to do something they didn't want to do, you would have threatened them with being sent back from where they'd fled in the first place.'

It fell silent for a moment, then Jack asked tentatively, 'If — and *only* if, mind — I could get Assistant Commissioner Bruce to agree to hire you, do you think you could stop this East End crime wave?'

'I could have a damned good stab at it,' Percy replied. 'But can you envisage the Met employing me to solve the crime that it exists to combat?'

'Not ordinarily, of course,' Jack conceded. 'But I think that things are getting pretty desperate.'

'If you could persuade Bruce, then of course I'd keep my price to a modest level,' Percy said. 'For old times' sake, if you like.'

'Before we get ahead of ourselves,' Esther cut in sternly, 'there's the matter that brought you here in the first place — the disappearance of Annabelle Pickering?'

'As I understand it,' Percy replied, 'you're waiting to be told when to leave the ransom money. Is that the case?'

'Yes. So what can we do in the meantime?' Esther asked.

'*You* can do very little,' Percy replied. 'Whereas *I* can continue my enquiries regarding who may be behind the entire business. And my first objective will be to learn more about the background of that man calling himself Stanley Pilgrim.'

CHAPTER NINE

Percy squinted hard as he tried to focus on the tiny wording visible in the light shining up through the microfilm from below. He was seated in a public room in the Public Record Office in Chancery Lane, risking his eyesight as he peered at the census record for 3rd April 1881 that recorded the presence at 35 Hewett Street, Shoreditch, of one Stanley Pilgrim, son of Walter Pilgrim, bootmaker. On that date Stanley's age was recorded as being twenty, and his occupation as that of 'apprentice bootmaker', no doubt apprenticed to his father in accordance with normal practice.

Also living in the house on that date was a younger son born to Walter and Clarice Pilgrim, named George, aged eighteen, and recorded as being 'not in employment'.

By the time of the 1891 census, George was twenty-eight, still living at the Hewett Street address, and giving his occupation as that of 'mariner'. This might cover either a career in Her Majesty's Navy, making him traceable through military records, or he could have become a merchant seaman, in which case Percy would need to learn which ships he'd been serving on at any particular time, or, if he got lucky, the shipping line by which he was employed.

The fact that the older brother, Stanley, was not listed as living in Hewett Street by 1891 tied in with what Jack had learned — namely that Stanley Pilgrim had died before then. Why, then, was he recorded as living in Hewett Street in April 1881 — a few weeks *after* his supposed death in March of that year?

Percy knew enough about census procedures to appreciate that it would have been consistent with the practice at that time to record the older son Stanley as 'ordinarily' living in Hewett Street and learning the boot-making trade, even if he was a serving soldier. The census records were officially only supposed to record those who were actually staying under the roof of each house on the night in question, but the forms from which the information was compiled were either self-authored, or — in the vast majority of those recorded in the East End — completed on the house occupier's behalf by clerks employed to collect either completed forms or the information to be entered on them. In other words, if the head of the house said that Stanley Pilgrim had been resident at 35 Hewett Street on 3rd April 1881, then officially he was, even though, unknown to his parents, he was already dead.

But what happened to his younger brother George? He would now be around thirty-six years of age, which might be true of the man Percy had interviewed the previous day. But what had he been doing since last recorded living in Hewett Street, Shoreditch in 1891? If he had adopted a life of crime, Jack could verify that by reference to criminal records. That would have to wait until tomorrow, unless Percy could shorten his enquiries by making use of a reliable local source closer to the house in question.

'I thought you'd bloody retired,' complained the desk sergeant on duty at Shoreditch Police Station that afternoon.

'So I did,' Percy replied. 'I am now a concerned citizen seeking the assistance of the local police in order to enquire whether my elderly sister, who does not enjoy the greatest of health, would be at risk in some way if, given her need to have her chimney swept, she employs one George Pilgrim, a man who claims to be a reliable and experienced chimneysweep.

She is frail and therefore vulnerable, and would be an easy target for robbery or worse, hence my enquiry.'

'And what makes you think that I can help?' the sergeant asked.

'You must know all there is to know about local families,' Percy replied, undeterred. 'And since the home address supplied by George Pilgrim is Hewett Street, which is barely a stone's throw from here, I thought you might be able to assist.'

The sergeant frowned. 'I only remember one George Pilgrim from around here,' he told Percy, 'and he was an unsuccessful fraud artist. Did a spell on board a timber ship out of Millwall Docks, then came back and started the "old soldier" routine, begging on street corners and pretending to be a wounded army hero with a busted leg. We nicked George a few times for vagrancy, and he was all set to do a lengthy spell as an "incorrigible rogue", as we call them in the trade, but the local vicar stepped in and kept him out of gaol. Haven't seen him around these parts in years, and don't want to. If I were you, I wouldn't let him near your sister's chimney, if it's the same man I'm thinking of.'

Percy beamed. 'Thank you, Sergeant. You've been most helpful.' He went back out into the street, convinced that the caretaker employed at Cassiobury House School was in fact one George Pilgrim, impersonating his dead older brother for reasons which perhaps only he knew. But that didn't provide any further clue as to who might have employed his talents in an endeavour to ruin the school, or indeed what motive they might have for seeking to do so.

'I wasn't expecting you home for tea, so you won't be getting any,' Beattie Enright told Percy as he threw his hat towards the peg on the back of the door. He missed, as usual.

'Fortunately, I was well fed by Jack and Esther,' Percy replied. 'They send their loving regards, by the way.'

'So, have you finished playing the hero for Esther?' Beattie demanded. 'Or are you hiding a tail between your legs because you got nowhere?'

'As a matter of fact, we're making good progress,' Percy replied.

'If you're making good progress in Watford, why are you back in Hackney after only a day away?'

'I spent most of the day in Shoreditch, as it happens, trying to trace someone who may now be posing as the caretaker in Esther's school. He has a somewhat shady past. So shady, in fact, that I could only find out that he was a deckhand on a timber ship for a while. Then he took to street begging, and was only saved from a spell in prison for vagrancy by the local God-botherer.'

Beattie pursed her lips. 'If by that blasphemous description you mean the local church minister, then I don't suppose it occurred to you to make enquiry of him?'

'What would be gained by that?'

'A good deal, perhaps,' Beattie replied. 'Church ministers do more than stand at the pulpit on Sundays, you know; they're responsible for the moral welfare of their flock. If the minister knew the man you're investigating well enough to speak for him in court, then perhaps he can point you in the direction of where he might be now.'

'It's worth a try, I suppose.'

'At least you'll be setting foot inside a church voluntarily,' said Beattie. 'And while you're there, see if you can't do something to preserve your own soul.'

'They were a tragic family in many ways,' the Reverend Tilney told Percy the following morning as they sat in the vestry of the local parish church in Shoreditch. 'They lost their elder son during the Boer War, as you may be aware, and the father died two years ago, they said of a broken heart. I presided over the funeral myself, given his years of devotion to this church. The mother, regrettably, found the loss of a son and husband too much for her fragile constitution, and she's now in St Luke's Hospital in Islington. I visit her whenever I can, although I don't believe she knows who I am anymore. So, why might you be seeking out George, Mr Enright?'

'The matter of an outstanding debt,' Percy hedged, in the belief that this sounded about right from what he knew of George Pilgrim.

The vicar made a disappointed sound. 'I had hoped that he'd changed his ways, but seemingly not. When he went to sea after the death of his older brother, whom he looked up to, we all hoped that it would be the making of him. But he abandoned that after a couple of years. Then, regrettably, he took to begging in the streets, pretending to be his wounded brother, returned from the Boer War. I was able to preserve him from a prison sentence by advising the magistrate of his tragic family history. Then a travelling fair set up in Middlesex Street in Spitalfields, where they now hold weekend markets, and I was fortunate to be able to supply him with a letter of introduction to the man who was running it and seeking labourers to help set up the attractions. I'm afraid I haven't heard of George, or *from* him, since.'

Percy was familiar with the Middlesex Street markets, better known to many as Petticoat Lane, and not in a good way. They used to say that if a house was burgled in the East End on a Saturday night, its contents would be offered for sale in Petticoat Lane on Sunday morning. It was a regular beat duty of police officers from Whitechapel, Shoreditch and Bethnal Green to raid the market stalls for stolen goods. The area was also rife with pickpockets and prostitutes, and it was totally in keeping with the opinion that Percy had formed of George Pilgrim that he would seek employment in some disreputable sideshow set up there temporarily.

Thanking the vicar warmly, to the extent of dropping ten shillings into the Poor Box near the front door of the church, Percy took a horse bus up to Euston, where he could catch the train to Watford in search of a free dinner and, hopefully, some further news of the missing girl he'd been called in to locate.

'Thank goodness you're back,' Esther greeted as Percy was shown into the living room of The Lodge, where she and Jack were enjoying a leisurely drink before dinner. 'We have an important development to report, and we need your advice on how best to deal with it. Whisky and soda?'

'That would be very nice, thank you,' Percy replied. 'I also have some news for you. The man claiming to be Stanley Pilgrim is almost certainly his younger brother George, who has a somewhat dubious background.'

'That makes sense,' said Jack, 'since the real Stanley Pilgrim has been dead for almost twenty years, hasn't he?'

'Correct,' Percy confirmed as he accepted the glass from Esther, took a sip, then sat down in the vacant chair opposite the settee on which Esther and Jack were seated. 'So what's your news?' he asked Esther.

'We've received the promised instructions regarding the handing over of the five thousand pounds,' she announced. 'It's to be tonight at ten o'clock, under the elm tree that sits just inside the copse of trees beyond the lawn. It's to be contained in a calico bag. Emily visited the bank during the lunch break between classes, and has the money ready to hand over.'

'Did the note say whether the girl — Annabelle, isn't it? — will be handed back unharmed in exchange?' Percy asked.

Esther shook her head. 'It didn't, and that's the first thing we need your advice on. Do we hand over the money without any guarantee that we'll get Annabelle back?'

Percy thought for a moment. 'We don't really have any choice, do we? But if we lie in wait for whoever collects the money, then put pressure on them to reveal the girl's whereabouts, we can hopefully find out where she's being held.'

'I have two objections,' Jack said. 'The first is that, for all we know, somebody has instructions to kill the girl, or at least silence her in some way if whoever is sent to collect the money doesn't return with it. The second is that by "we" you presumably mean you and I?'

'I do,' Percy replied. 'I suggest that Emily should remain at her upstairs bedroom window, since I gather from what she has told me that she can see the entire lawn and copse area from there. She can keep her window open and shout out if there's any sign of a double-cross.'

'Then who's going to deliver the money?' Esther asked.

'I was hoping you'd volunteer. It has to be someone from the school, and in the darkness you might even be mistaken for Emily, although it doesn't matter whether you are or not. They'll expect you to be guarded by someone, and Jack is the obvious person to do that. I'll lurk in the shadows, then when Jack pounces on whoever collects the money, I'll either join in or fight off anyone else who's been sent to do the double-cross.'

'By *double-cross*, you mean a failure to produce Annabelle?' Jack asked.

Percy nodded. 'Yes, either that or a concerted attack on you and Esther. That's more likely if Esther is mistaken for Emily, because the more I enquire into this case, the more convinced I am that she's the real target, rather than the school.'

Jack frowned. 'So, we've got no guarantee that Annabelle will be handed over in exchange for the money, we don't know who is really behind all this, and it all seems to depend upon you or I catching whoever comes to collect the money. Is this a good idea, Uncle?'

'Do you have a better plan?' Percy asked, and Jack shook his head. 'Then we go with the one I just outlined,' Percy went on. 'Now, presumably I haven't missed dinner? Your Aunt Beattie was less than generous with breakfast, although the obvious advantage in that was that I didn't spend the day doubled up with wind.'

The church clock chimed ten as furtive shadows took up their places in the school grounds. Emily was standing guard by her open bedroom window, the light off, staring down at the top of Percy's head as he pressed himself up against the front wall of the school. He in turn was watching Esther and Jack walking down to the elm tree and carrying the calico bag in which was deposited five thousand pounds in notes of large denomination. The atmosphere was tense, and the silence of the night made everything seem eerie as Esther and Jack approached the elm and laid the bag down beneath its spreading lower branches.

Suddenly a voice cried out from the darkness.

'I'm here!' The faint outline of a girl could be seen at the far end of the school wall, presumably waiting to be rescued. Esther gave a sharp cry and raced towards her, while Jack made a futile effort to call her back in case it was a trap, then ran after her when she ignored him. The girl disappeared from sight just as Esther reached the front wall of the school, and at that moment Percy was felled by a heavy blow from behind.

Jack reached a bewildered-looking Esther as she peered into the darkness towards Pilgrim's hut. 'She's gone,' she said miserably. 'I was sure it was Annabelle, but perhaps I was just *hoping* that it was.'

'Presumably the money has gone, too,' Jack added gloomily. 'It looks as if Percy was right. The figure was a diversion and we've been outwitted.'

'Where *is* he, anyway?' Esther asked.

They both looked back towards where they knew Percy to have been concealed. An indistinct form was bending over a bundle on the ground. As they hurried over, they realised that it was Percy, clutching the back of his head and being comforted by Emily.

'I didn't see who did it,' Emily admitted. 'I just became aware of Percy falling in a heap and I rushed down as fast as I could.'

'We were tricked into believing that Annabelle had returned,' Esther told her. 'But whoever it was has disappeared, and we believe that the money will have been taken.'

'I'll go and check,' Jack volunteered, as Percy rose unsteadily to his feet.

'Jack won't be the only Enright with an extra head by tomorrow morning,' he muttered. 'But let's make a search of the grounds, just in case.'

'You're going nowhere in that condition,' Emily insisted. 'Come inside and I'll make you some tea.'

'What's goin' on out 'ere?' came a rough enquiry and Pilgrim appeared, armed with the same club that he claimed to have found on the ground the night that Jack had been hit on the head.

At that moment Jack returned. 'The bag's disappeared, as we suspected,' he said. He glared at Pilgrim. 'What are you doing out here?' he demanded.

'I 'eard a girl callin' out, didn't I?' the caretaker replied. 'Who were that?'

'Never mind,' Emily replied sternly. 'Just go back to your quarters — this has nothing to do with you.'

'Right bloody carry-on,' Pilgrim muttered as he walked away.

'I suppose I'd better call the police,' Emily said quietly.

'Is that really necessary?' Esther asked. 'Why don't we wait until tomorrow morning and then tell them the whole story? Annabelle hasn't been returned to us, and we have to assume the worst.'

'You may be right,' Emily conceded sadly. 'I'll go upstairs and put the pan on for some tea.'

CHAPTER TEN

'I hope they don't think we're a fairground sideshow,' Percy muttered as he and Jack made their way to the front desk of Watford Police Station the following morning. 'Please give a warm welcome to The Double-Headed Enrights!'

'The lump will go down in a few days, if it's anything like mine,' Jack reassured him as he rang the bell on the desk.

A sergeant emerged from the office. 'You again!' he muttered when he caught sight of Jack. 'I've been told to apologise to you for my manner when you last came here. I didn't realise that you were high up in the Met.'

'It shouldn't have mattered *who* I was,' Jack protested, 'but this time I'm going to insist that you do something about what I have to report, namely a girl who's been missing for almost a week now. This gentleman with me is an enquiry agent hired to find her, so far without success.'

'Thank you for the reminder,' Percy muttered under his breath, as Jack pressed on.

'Are you still the senior man here? Or have you acquired an inspector since I last visited?'

'We have, as it happens,' the sergeant replied as he waved to a uniformed constable who'd just walked in. 'Constable Bevan, could you please ask the inspector to come down here?'

A few minutes later, a stern-looking man appeared. 'I'm Inspector Bradbury,' he announced. He was wearing what was obviously a recently acquired — and somewhat tight — uniform as he made his way down the stairs to the front desk. 'I'm told that a girl is missing. Are you a concerned parent?'

'No,' Jack replied, 'I'm the husband of the deputy headmistress of the school from which the girl disappeared several days ago. Cassiobury House School, down Rickmansworth Road and across from the Cassiobury estate.'

'Several *days* ago?' the inspector echoed. 'Why have you left it until now to report it? I would have thought that someone of your rank within the Yard would have been the first to engage all the resources of a modern police force. But of course, you lack recent operational experience, do you not, stuck behind an administration desk?'

'Perhaps he does, but *I* don't!' Percy snapped. 'I retired from Scotland Yard at a rank higher than yours, and *all* my years were spent operationally. It was my decision to refrain from calling in the local force, and from what I've heard of your competence, that was a wise decision. So I suggest that we dispense with the insults and chest-beating and get on with finding this child!'

'From where was she taken, did you say?' Bradbury asked, clearly swallowing his resentment.

'From the school, during the lunch break,' Jack told him. 'We believe that she was seized from the edge of a copse that fringes the school grounds, and has open land on the other side. There's nothing to suggest that she cried out for help, and there were other children nearby — my own daughter included — so it's possible that she was either drugged or rendered unconscious. The school has received a ransom note, demanding five thousand pounds for her release. The note said not to involve the police and, of course, our first thought was for her welfare. However, when we handed over the money, we were tricked into believing that the girl had been released, only she hadn't. Our concern now is that whoever is still holding her has nothing to gain by keeping her alive. That's why we're now coming to you for assistance, since you can mount the sort of search that we can't.'

'I'll need a full description of the girl, obviously, and details of when and where she was last seen,' Bradbury replied.

'I have all that written down here,' Jack replied as he removed a sheet of paper from his jacket.

'You might also wish to advise the local newspaper,' Percy added. 'Tell them that whoever is behind this business tried to persuade the proprietor and headmistress that the girl had been taken by a ghost that's rumoured to haunt the school. It was clearly designed to frighten the pupils, and will give the reading public some idea of how devious and determined whoever is behind this really is. It's clearly some sort of vendetta aimed at either the school itself or the lady who purchased it.'

'Very well,' Bradbury agreed. 'Now, if there's nothing else, I need to set the wheels in motion.'

Jack and Percy left the station. 'So what do we do now?' Jack asked as they stood outside in the sunlight.

'We wait,' Percy replied. 'Or, at least, you do. I think it's time I turned my talents towards ending this crime wave in the East End. You might wish to enquire of Assistant Commissioner Bruce whether it might be worth a thousand pounds to him.'

'The suggestion is outrageous!' Assistant Commissioner Bruce spluttered when Jack put the idea to him three days later. 'You say that a man of your acquaintance can singlehandedly put a stop to a crime wave in the East End that has lasted for well over two years, and has defeated all the resources of the Met? Is he certifiably insane, or have you run out of fresh ideas?'

'I'm simply passing on what he told me,' Jack muttered, acutely embarrassed. 'I can just as easily tell him that you're not interested.'

'You can certainly tell him that,' Bruce boomed. 'And you can also tell me how this man was able to contact a senior member of the Yard with an offer to do our job for us. It concerns me greatly that some arrogant fool thinks that he can wade in like some sort of knight on a charger and achieve alone what five police divisions have proved incapable of doing. Who *is* this man?'

'I'm not at liberty to say, sir,' Jack replied, his head bowed.

'It's Percy bloody Enright, isn't it?'

'As I said, sir, I'm not at liberty to say.'

'Well, you can tell your uncle from me that if I catch a single whiff of him interfering with policing in the East End, I'll have him up on a charge so fast that his retirement years will be spent staring through the bars of a cell in Newgate. Is that clear, Chief Inspector?'

'I'll certainly pass that message on, sir.'

It was not to be the only verbal roasting that Jack received that day. He was barely through the front door on his return home when he caught sight of Esther in the doorway to the sitting room, hands on her hips.

'What in God's name did you think you were about?' she snapped.

'When?'

'When you and Percy went down to the local police station to enlist their help in finding Annabelle. Which of you geniuses came up with the idea of informing the newspapers?'

'That was Percy —'

Esther cut him off. 'And you did nothing to stop him?'

'Why would I? We need all the publicity we can get in locating Annabelle.'

'Well, you *certainly* got a lot of publicity!' Esther cried. 'It's all over the papers that the school's haunted by the ghost of a woman who steals children, that all the other children are in terror of being the next to be seized, and that there are fears that the girl already stolen will be found dead somewhere in the grounds, which is why the police have been trampling through it for the past day or two. Five more children have been withdrawn from the school, leaving Primary One with just five pupils — one of whom is my own daughter — and Annabelle's father has instructed lawyers to sue the school for neglect of care. On top of that, a newspaper hound from London even managed to conduct an interview with Annabelle's mother, who — and I quote — "spoke through her tears of the day that a wicked ghost from three centuries in the past stole her only reason for living." Really helpful, wasn't it?'

Jack sighed. 'We meant well, and acted with the best of motives,' he said. 'We'll take steps to advise the newspapers that matters have become grossly exaggerated.'

'You'll go nowhere near the newspapers, do you understand?' Esther said firmly. 'The last thing we need is a quotation in the next edition from the husband of Cassiobury House School's deputy headmistress who claims that matters have got out of hand!'

'If you say so,' Jack muttered.

'I *do* say so!' Esther replied sharply. 'And you can tell Percy that he's no longer welcome here!'

The following morning, shortly after nine, Rufus Tomkins looked up from his desk in the outer office above the candle shop on Devonshire Road as an irate Jack Enright threw open the door with such determination that it banged hard against the wall.

'I want to see Percy Enright — *now*!' he demanded.

'He's not in,' Rufus said.

'He's my uncle,' Jack told him.

'He's still not in.'

'Then I'll wait until he is,' Jack insisted.

'Actually,' Rufus admitted, 'he told me that he'll be out on enquiries until after lunch, so you might be in for a long wait.'

'Then I'll leave a message,' Jack said, 'and you might want to write this down. Tell him that Jack Enright called, that he's annoyed with the mess that Percy's caused, and that he's no longer welcome in our house. Did you get that down?'

'I think I'll remember it,' Rufus said, 'or at least the sentiment involved. It's not what we're accustomed to hearing from grateful clients.'

'I'm surprised to learn that you have any!' Jack retorted as he turned and left the outer office, slamming the door hard behind him. A few moments later the door to the inner office opened a few inches, and Percy's face appeared in the crack.

'Did you get that, sir?' Rufus asked with a smirk.

'Loud and clear. It looks as if I need to start working towards my redemption.'

It was business as usual inside the White Hart in Whitechapel High Street. But the 'business' that it conducted was hardly that which the local chamber of commerce would have approved. Most of the clientele were thieves, drug dealers and bully boys, and they could be found perched on stools at the long bar with its brass rail, or grouped around tables loaded with drinks. A gin-soddened lady plinked out the latest popular tunes on a piano that had several of its keys missing, while keeping a watchful eye on her team of prostitutes who were seeking 'marks' among the more smartly dressed men.

They could hardly have been expected to notice the portly middle-aged man in the brown bowler hat with its green feather, who blended in with the more dapper of those seeking refreshment that evening. But one man noticed him, because he'd been told to look out for him.

'Mr Percival?' the man asked as he slid onto a bar stool alongside him. 'What's your poison?'

'If you're Mr Moses,' Percy replied, 'then it's a whisky and soda. If you're not, go away and mind your own business.'

'I'm Max Moses,' the man replied. He snapped his fingers and the bar attendant ran the length of the bar in order not to displease one of the most feared men in Whitechapel. 'I'm told that you have some information of value for me.'

'Who told you that I was looking for you?' asked Percy. 'You'll appreciate that the nature of my business is such that there can be no mistakes.'

'It was Lemmy Cohen, and the only mistake you're in danger of making is not getting to the point.'

'Very well, you know my name,' Percy replied. 'What you now need to know is that I run a private enquiry agency.'

'I see. Well, my wife knows all about Clara Solomons,' Moses replied, 'so if you're after blackmail money, then your luck just ran out. I only have to raise my hand and you'll be found up a back alley with your throat slit.'

'This has nothing to do with your mistress. I've been consulted by the Home Office in Whitehall. They're concerned about all the folk coming into the East End from parts of Russia.'

'Tell me something I *don't* know,' Moses growled. 'I'm rapidly running out of patience.'

'Well, what you probably don't know is that the Home Office have been approached by the Russian government. Apparently they don't take kindly to allegations that they were persecuting Jews, particularly in a place called Moldova, and they'd like to have some "meaningful conversations" with those refugees they claim have been spreading those "lies".'

'So?'

'So, I was hired to seek out those who have been identified as being what you might call "criminal elements".'

Moses gave an ironic laugh. 'Do me a favour. Do you imagine that we all sell Bibles for a living?'

'Far from it, which is why I thought it might be worth my while to let you know who's been pointing the finger at you and your business associates as suitable persons to be rounded up and sent back to Moldova.'

'And who's that?'

'What's it worth?'

'It's worth your life,' Moses snarled.

'Ever heard of Manny Jacobs?'

'Was it him?'

'I'll tell you if it was him in exchange for a hundred quid.'

'I don't think you quite understand how I do business, Mr Percival, or whatever your real name is. You tell me in exchange for your life, and — if I'm feeling generous — another whisky and soda.'

'On that understanding, it was indeed Manny Jacobs. He asked for a meeting with me after I was hired by the Home Office, and he pointed me down here. He told me that the

Bessarabian Tigers have been terrorising Whitechapel for the past two years and that I could find their leader — you, Mr Moses — through his second-in-command, Lemmy Cohen.'

'You've earned another whisky and soda, Mr Percival,' said Moses. 'But if you repeat one word of this conversation to anyone, we'll find you and rip your throat out. Understood?'

A few minutes later Percy was safely back out in Whitechapel High Street, and heaving great sighs of relief. Meanwhile, Moses was issuing instructions to one of his so-called "enforcement" teams, who would shortly be making a visit to Bethnal Green, adequately equipped with firearms and volatile fluid.

CHAPTER ELEVEN

'You have an opportunity to redeem yourself,' Esther announced when she met Jack at the front door.

'Which dragon do I have to slay?' he asked, almost resigned to the silent treatment of the last week.

'We're taking the pupils to the circus on Saturday,' she told him, 'and Emily said that it would be a good idea to have a police escort.'

'All of them?' he asked.

Esther nodded. 'Thanks to you and Percy we have less than a dozen students left, including Lily, and when she announced that she would be going, Bertie, Miriam and Tommy made such a fuss that I agreed that they could come along as well. We're hiring our own horse bus as the big top will be set up in Clarence Park in St Albans, which is ten miles away.'

'There used to be a circus every year in Victoria Park when I lived with Percy and Beattie,' Jack reminisced. 'I used to imagine myself as the lion tamer.'

'You obviously settled for the clown role,' Esther observed tartly, and Jack opted not to push his luck.

'How did you find out about the circus, anyway?' he asked.

'The promoters — Billings' Circus — pushed one of their promotions broadsheets into the school letterbox, and Emily thought that it would be a nice treat for the pupils after the stressful time they've had recently. All the parents have signed notes confirming their consent, but Emily thought it would be better if we could show that we had a police officer in attendance.'

'I haven't dared ask how things are going at the school,' Jack ventured. 'Have any more parents removed their children?'

'No, thank goodness, although Emily fears that any day now she'll be served with legal papers from Annabelle's father.'

'And no news of Annabelle, I assume? You *would* have told me, if there had been?'

'Of course I would. Anyway, Emily's booked tickets for this coming Saturday. The bus will leave the school at midday and the show is in the afternoon. We can have a late breakfast, and Emily's arranging for Mrs Finch to pack picnics for all the pupils.'

When Saturday arrived, Esther and Jack shepherded their four children safely across Rickmansworth Road and into Park Avenue, where the horse bus was already waiting in the school grounds. Emily and Esther loaded the excited pupils into it, instructing them to be on their best behaviour during the trip up the road north to St Albans, and the field that lay to the east of the town centre.

The tickets that Emily had purchased for the show put them in the first two rows of seats directly in front of the action.

First out were the clowns, throwing buckets of water over each other, hurling custard pies into each other's faces, and generally setting a light-hearted tone for what was to follow. Jack noted with interest that one of the clowns was a woman, and their act had been devised in such a way that she always got the better of her two fellow performers, gaining her the loudest laughter and applause.

The first of the main acts consisted of a family group of acrobats, and Esther thought she recognised them from the fair held in Cassiobury Park some weeks earlier. Then came a parade of elephants, followed by a couple of performing horses that bowed to the audience before taking their leave of the ring.

Then the ringmaster appeared. 'For a few heart-stopping moments the Flying Giraldos will defy gravity and send your pulses cart-wheeling as they soar fifty feet above the sawdust,' he announced. 'While the circus hands are setting up the ropes and trapezes, please welcome back Lazy, Daisy and Pasty.'

The three clowns skipped back out into the centre of the ring, and before long Lazy and Pasty were chasing Daisy round in circles with buckets of red paint, which they somehow always seem to miss splattering her with. Finally, in a cheeky act of defiance, Daisy, who was dressed in a ballgown that trailed in the sawdust, turned her back on her pursuers and glided quickly away through the back entrance. It was impossible to see her feet under the gown, but she moved as if she was on roller skates.

Jack felt a chill run up his spine as he recognised the gliding motion as that of the ghost he'd seen crossing the grass at the school, just before he'd been whacked over the head. He looked back into the second row, towards Emily, who stared back at him with her mouth open. Clearly she'd recognised the similarity as well.

Whatever 'heart-stopping' acrobatics the Flying Giraldos performed were lost on Jack as he contemplated the possibility that the ghost of Lady Anne had been manufactured by Billings' Circus. When their act ended, and while the circus hands removed the trapezes and dangling ropes ahead of the next act, which promised to be a sword swallower, a group of children dressed as toy soldiers stepped into the ring and began marching up and down in time to a rousing tune from the circus musicians, a trio that had been stoically providing a melodic backdrop to the entire show.

Suddenly, all thoughts of the ghost were driven from Jack's mind when Lily, seated with the other children between Jack and Esther, suddenly gasped, 'There's Annabelle!'

Jack had never met Annabelle, but when he looked at Esther, he could tell by her transfixed stare that she'd formed the same conclusion. She leaned back into the second row and said something to Emily, who nodded, and then appeared to give way to tears.

Esther leaned across the children and asked Jack, 'What can we do?'

Despite being severely tempted to race forward and grab whichever of the children had been identified as the missing Annabelle, Jack managed to suppress the instinct. 'Nothing at the moment,' he replied. 'At least we know that she's still alive and, from the smile on her face, perhaps wasn't abducted against her will after all.'

The rest of the show, with its dancing ponies, jugglers and frequent performances from the clowns, passed painfully slowly. The children's dance troupe didn't reappear until the very end, joining all the other performers in a final bow to bring the show to a close.

The return journey in the horse bus seemed to take forever, but they finally reached the junction of Rickmansworth Road with Park Avenue, where Jack and Esther's own children were dropped off at The Lodge, to be fed an early tea by Polly and Alice. They remained on the bus as it returned to the school grounds, where parents were waiting to take the remaining pupils home. Emily invited Jack and Esther upstairs to her apartment, and put the pan on to boil for tea. 'That was definitely Annabelle, and I don't think I've ever seen her smiling so broadly. I'm uncertain now whether she was taken against her will, and we can't just blunder back to the circus with the police and demand that they hand her over. It's all very difficult.'

'How well do you know Annabelle's father?' Jack ventured.

'Hardly at all,' Emily replied. 'I only met him and his wife for the first time when they signed Annabelle up as a pupil. Why do you ask?'

'Well, suppose he devised the entire business in order to obtain five thousand pounds?'

Emily shook her head. 'He's a very successful businessman, with interests in both shipping and theatres,' she said.

'We need to speak to Annabelle without anyone else around,' Esther concluded. 'That way, we can ask her whether she's there of her own free will, or if she's too frightened to attempt an escape.'

'I can think of only one person who might be able to come up with a strategy for talking to Annabelle privately, and learning the truth,' said Jack. 'But he's banned from our house.'

'If you're referring to your incorrigible Uncle Percy, I might be able to tolerate him just once more,' Esther conceded. 'But *only* once.'

'What's he done wrong?' Emily asked.

'What's he done *right*?' Esther retorted. 'He bungled the handing over of five thousand pounds that you could ill afford to lose, and then he made a complete mess of speaking to the newspapers, and, well, isn't that enough?'

'I don't think you can blame him solely for those misfortunes,' Emily cautioned. 'I had formed a rather higher opinion of his abilities than that.'

'Not as high as his own opinion of himself,' Esther countered. 'You wouldn't believe the scrapes he's got us into over the years — me especially.'

'But he's very useful when the circumstances call for subterfuge,' Jack reminded her. 'Don't forget how he managed to prove, against all the odds, that a West End art dealer had pushed his sister off a train in Wiltshire.'

'And may *I* remind *you* that he only did so by employing your own sister to pose as a ghost, and exposing me to danger when I was talked into working as his bookkeeper,' Esther fired back.

'I don't deny any of that,' Jack replied, 'but in the absence of any other way forward, I think we should try and persuade him to help us speak to Annabelle.'

'Do you think he'll need persuading?' Emily asked.

Jack nodded firmly. 'After the message I left for him at his office when Esther banned him from the house, I think he'll need at least a grovelling apology.'

'Well, he won't be getting one from me,' Esther stated.

'Perhaps I could talk him round?' Emily suggested.

Jack shook his head. 'This requires another Enright,' he announced, 'and one who knows Uncle Percy's greatest weakness.'

This time Jack opened the office door in Devonshire Street with the respect to which it was entitled. When Rufus Tomkins looked up apprehensively from his papers, Jack treated him to a warm smile.

'Please tell Percy that his nephew Jack would like to buy him lunch at a certain chophouse of his acquaintance on the Embankment. Twelve noon. Today. Thank you.'

Jack looked up three hours later as Percy approached the table in Tang Li's Chophouse that had been a home from home for them both during a previous investigation. Percy, for his part, kept a straight face as he asked, 'Has the excommunication been lifted, and may I once again regard myself as *persona grata* in the Watford household?'

'It was Esther with the bell, book and candle, let me assure you,' Jack replied as he waved him into the vacant seat. 'She was far from impressed by the way the newspapers handled the story you gave them regarding Annabelle's disappearance. But now we've found the girl, and we need your help.'

'Three things,' Percy replied as he studied the menu card. 'First of all, is it my fault if the press never let the truth get in the way of a good story? Secondly, and more to the point, if you've found Annabelle, why do you need me? And thirdly, have you decided what you're having, or will you join me in a meat pie?'

'Would there be room for both of us?' Jack joked, then wished he hadn't when he saw Percy's mouth set in disapproval. 'Yes — meat pie sounds good.'

'So, why are my services required?' Percy asked.

'Well, quite by coincidence we saw Annabelle performing in a circus in St Albans,' Jack explained. 'She seemed very happy, so there's now some doubt as to whether or not she was abducted. What we need is some ruse whereby we can speak to her and enquire if she's there voluntarily, or if she needs to be rescued.'

'And you couldn't work one out for yourselves — is that the case?'

'Please don't go all superior on me, Uncle,' Jack pleaded. 'We really *do* need your help, and you're without peer when it comes to devious behaviour.'

'Flattery will get you part of the way,' Percy said. 'But may I assume that Assistant Commissioner Bruce rejected my entirely reasonable terms for ridding the East End of its Russian gangs? If he'd accepted, I would have expected to hear from you earlier. As it transpires, I've already set to work, and the results have been rather gratifying.'

'In what way?'

Percy gave a loud tut. 'Do you no longer read the overnight crime reports?'

'Of course I do,' Jack assured him, 'but which of those are you taking credit for?'

'The little matter of the fire-bombing of a house in Bishops Way, Bethnal Green. The former home of one Emmanuel Jacobs, leader of the Odessian gang that think they rule the roost down there. Subsequently, by a coincidence that would almost be considered divine had it not been engineered by a private enquiry agent sitting not far from you now, the White Hart pub in Whitechapel was attacked the following day, immediately after closing time, and several leading members of the Bessarabian Tigers were wounded by way of reprisal from members of the very irate Odessians. The festivities seem destined to continue until they've wiped each other out.'

Jack raised an eyebrow. 'So, you set one gang against another?' he asked. 'How exactly did you achieve that?'

'Simple, Jack. As I already explained to you and Esther recently, you find what it is that criminals most fear, and then you threaten them with it if they don't desist from their criminal activities. But in the case of these two gangs I had to be a bit more direct, since subtlety is not one of their strong suits. I posed as a man with inside knowledge from the Home Office and told the leader of the Bessarabians that the Odessians had secretly identified them as suitable for deportation back to Moldova. Then I said precisely the same to the leader of the Odessians. They proved to be quite unforgiving on both sides. You might want to inform Assistant

Commissioner Bruce that there will be further bodies for collection in the coming weeks.'

'I don't think you'll get your thousand pounds,' Jack said.

'Then I'll take satisfaction in a job well done,' Percy replied. 'Now, tell me what it is, precisely, that you want from me.'

Jack explained that they needed some strategy by which they could single out Annabelle at the circus in order to enquire whether or not she was there voluntarily. 'Can we make a start this evening?' he asked hopefully.

'Regrettably not,' Percy replied. 'This evening I have an appointment at a certain hotel in Belgravia, where the wife of a prominent peer of the realm is planning on taking her much younger lover for a night of unbridled passion. I shall be playing the role of the room service waiter who can later confirm their joint occupancy of the same bedroom.'

'Her husband is paying your fee, presumably?'

'They both are,' Percy said. 'They each, for their own reasons, wish to divorce, and what they are inclined to refer to in court as "standard hotel evidence" will do the trick. Regrettably, it has to be the lady who appears to sin, because under the current law only the husband may seek a divorce on the grounds of adultery. The young man in question will also be well remunerated, I have no doubt. So, it will have to be tomorrow, I'm afraid.'

'You asked to see me, sir?' Jack asked as he stood hesitantly in the doorway to Assistant Commissioner Bruce's office that afternoon.

'Ah yes, come in.' Bruce beckoned Jack into his office. 'You've presumably heard about this recent slaughter in the East End?'

'In Whitechapel and Bethnal Green? Yes, sir,' Jack replied, glad of his choice of lunch companion two hours earlier.

'A very smart tactic on the part of the person who you were not at liberty to name, and for as long as the members of those criminal gangs carry on killing each other we won't interfere. But you can tell Percy that he's not getting his thousand.'

'As I already said, sir —' Jack began, but Bruce cut him short.

'Yes, I know, you're not at liberty to divulge his identity. But you can tell him that his efforts have not gone unnoticed. That'll be all.'

The following evening a hat appeared round the front door of The Lodge, attached to Percy's hand.

'If you want to take aim now,' came Percy's voice from the other side of the door, 'then at least I'll only lose my hand, and not my head.'

'Come in, Percy, and stop playing around!' Esther replied in a commanding voice. 'There's whisky and soda on offer in the sitting room, since Jack considers that I owe you an apology, and lamb chops for supper because I *definitely* owe Jack one, after the way he's carried your sins on his shoulders for the past week or so.'

Esther smiled despite herself, and the ice appeared to have been broken as they sat down to eat shortly afterwards.

'So, have you formed any ideas yet that we can consider, Uncle?' Jack asked as he carved into his lamb chop.

'From what you told me yesterday,' Percy replied, 'Annabelle appears to be a member of a troupe of children that perform as dancers in a travelling circus. That being the case, one has to speculate regarding their education — whether or not it exists, and if so, the quality of it.'

'That's a very valid point,' Esther told them. 'Show people obviously move from place to place, and therefore their children aren't registered with a particular school. The law requires all children to attend school until they're eleven years old, but following negotiations with nomadic folk such as circus promoters, Romany travellers and those who take their services around the country, like knife grinders, the government settled for an arrangement under which children could be educated on the road, as it were. Unfortunately, there's no effective way of checking whether that education is being provided at all.'

'Do they send school inspectors out to check on that?' Percy asked.

Esther shrugged. 'Whenever possible, but as you'll appreciate, it's pretty piecemeal and uneven.'

'So, it would not be unusual for an education inspector, along with a teacher, to visit this circus and speak with all the children, testing their level of learning?'

'If you have in mind what I *think* you have in mind, I would need to be that teacher, since only I could adequately assess what teaching they've received.'

Percy sat back with a broad smile. 'Let it be placed on the record that this time Esther Enright *volunteered* to assist in one of my schemes without even being asked.'

'So, we'll single out each child until we get to Annabelle, then ask her if she was abducted or not?' Jack asked.

Percy shook his head. 'For once you'll take a back seat, Jack. If we need official police involvement then we can always call in the local lot. But we'd lack credibility if we approached the circus as education inspectors with you in tow.'

'And that's *you* put in your place,' Esther said, smiling. 'Anyone for date pudding?'

CHAPTER TWELVE

'We got a visit from you lot only a couple of months ago,' Norman Billings protested when Percy and Esther presented themselves as education inspectors at the circus of which he was the ringmaster.

'And where were you located at that time?' Percy asked, undeterred.

'Surrey. Godalming, to be precise.'

'Different county,' Percy replied. 'So, if we might begin with the oldest child, and work down through the age levels, Miss Jacobs here will administer certain basic tests.'

Two hours later, Esther was forced to concede that the children's education levels were satisfactory. 'But we've yet to see Annabelle,' she said.

'Leave it to me,' Percy muttered. He went in search of Billings and found him quickly. 'We believe that there may be other children living here that we haven't yet seen,' he told the ringmaster, who looked startled for a moment.

'You've seen them all. Anna Giraldo was the last — the remainder are all younger than five, which, as you'll be aware, is the minimum age at which children are to be provided with an education.'

'You haven't recruited any children recently, while you've been here in Hertfordshire?'

'Definitely not,' Billings insisted. 'The last to join us were the two twins who belong to the sword swallower, Jack Campbell, and you've already seen them.'

'If you say so,' Percy conceded. 'That being the case, I'm pleased to be able to tell you that Miss Jacobs is more than satisfied with the educational standards that she found here, and we'll take our leave.'

As they made their way out of the field and back to the waiting coach that they'd hired for the day, they noticed the son of the elephant handler approaching Billings, their heads close together in a whispered conversation.

A despondent Percy and Esther returned to The Lodge and reported to Jack that there had been no sign of Annabelle during their visit to the circus.

'I need to get back to the school tomorrow,' Esther reminded them. 'I can't expect Emily to teach two classes for more than one day.'

'So, what do we do next?' Jack asked.

Percy appeared to be thinking. 'Annabelle was *definitely* seen with the group of dancers?' he asked. 'There can be no mistake about that?'

'Absolutely not,' replied Esther. 'It was Lily who drew our attention to her, and once she did, both Emily and myself were convinced that it was her.'

'So, we must assume that the circus people are keeping her hidden away,' Percy concluded. 'Which raises the possibility that she is being held against her will. If we could somehow get a message to her that it's safe to make a run for it, with police officers standing by to ensure that she gets away without interference from anyone at the circus, would that work?'

Esther nodded. 'It might. There were uniformed officers in the vicinity during the Saturday afternoon performance that we attended, keeping an eye on the crowd as they queued for admission. So they wouldn't look unusual or out of place.' Then a thought struck her. 'What about Lily? She's Annabelle's friend. If we could somehow get Lily alongside her, we might at least find out if she wants to leave the circus, in which case the two of you could provide her with a safe escort.'

'So it's just a matter of getting Lily in there somehow,' Jack said.

Esther grinned. 'Would anyone notice an extra person in that dance troupe of youngsters, given that it must be total chaos behind the scenes when they're changing acts?'

It felt silent, until Jack and Percy said, simultaneously, 'Lily?'

'Yes, why not?' Esther said. 'She doesn't need to be able to dance. All she needs to do is join the line of children waiting to go into the ring, dressed in the same sort of costume, and pull Annabelle to one side. If the two of you are hanging around the back at the same time, disguised as circus hands, you can then escort her away —assuming that she wants to leave. You can also alert the uniformed constables to be prepared to wade in if needed.'

'How can you ensure that Lily will look the part?' Percy asked.

'You're talking to an experienced seamstress, remember — one whose abilities you have employed on more than one occasion in the past,' Esther replied, raising her eyebrows. 'And Lily has a good eye for costume, so between us we can probably devise something that looks about right. It won't need to undergo detailed scrutiny — it just needs to look passable for a few minutes in the half light of the circus wings. All the better if we choose an evening performance. I just hope that the circus doesn't move on in the meantime.'

Esther's faith in Lily was confirmed when the idea was put to her the following morning, and together they set to work creating a reproduction of the toy soldier costume that they both recalled from their circus visit the previous week. Percy, meanwhile, was sent to meet with Emily at the school and advise her of what was being planned. He also had to inform her, with regret, that she would be teaching both classes for another day. When Jack returned home from work that evening, he was met by an excited Lily, dressed like a toy soldier.

'From what you remember of that troupe of young dancers, could you spot this costume as a fake?' Esther asked him eagerly.

'You're asking the wrong person,' Jack replied. 'Fake banknotes are more in my line, but to my untutored eye it looks about right.'

'That's just as well,' Esther replied, 'because we'll be putting it to the test this evening. Your supper's on the table, then you have work to do. You *and* Percy, who's already eaten.'

'We'll be right behind you,' Jack assured Lily as she stood nervously waiting for the young dancers to appear in their toy soldier costumes. Jack certainly looked the part of a circus hand, with his gardening trousers over a pair of well-worn boots, and an old waistcoat with egg stains down the front that Esther had retrieved from the dustbin. Percy, who did not have a change of clothes, had nevertheless done his bit by discarding his jacket and rolling up his shirt sleeves. He looked more like a bar attendant in a public house, but would pass for a circus hand in the faint light of the entrance to the big top that the performers used.

There was an anxious moment while a line of elephants was led back out into the grassy area to the rear of the big top, then the young dancers began to gather ahead of their scheduled performance. Suddenly Lily leapt forward and grabbed one of the dancers by the arm.

'Annabelle!' she cried. 'Where have you been all this time? We've been looking for you *everywhere*! Do you want to come home with me?'

'Who are you?' demanded a burly youth who appeared to be leading the troupe. 'Leave Annie alone — we're due on in a few moments!'

Jack and Percy moved into place behind Lily, who pointed at Jack.

'This is my Papa, Annabelle, and this other man is his uncle. Do you want to come home with us now?'

'Your home, yes — not mine,' Annabelle whispered anxiously, just as the ringmaster could be heard calling in the dancers. The youth who'd challenged Lily turned to glare at Annabelle as the tent flaps were pulled back, and then the dancers ran out into the ring.

'Come with us, quickly!' Lily urged Annabelle, and all four of them ran round the back of the big top to the stand where the tickets were sold, which was now empty of circus staff, but attended by two uniformed police officers.

'I'm Enright, and so's he,' Percy told the two officers, 'and you can stand down once you see us safely into that coach waiting in the road.' Then they all ran as hard as they could until they reached the coach in which Esther was waiting for them. Lily and Jack helped Annabelle to climb in, then Esther pulled her into a warm embrace.

Percy jumped up onto the running board alongside the coach driver and gave the command for the return to Watford.

'Don't spare the horses,' he added. The driver gave him a curious look, to which Percy responded, 'I've always wanted to say that.'

Inside the coach, as it swayed and bumped its way back south, Annabelle had begun to cry softly. Lily, holding her hand, reassured her that she was safe. 'Mama's here, and she's happy to see you again. We *all* are, and you're not in any trouble. Once we get home, you can tell us all about your adventures.'

An hour later, as they sat around the kitchen table, Annabelle whispered to Lily, 'Will we be getting something to eat? Only I missed tonight's show, so I won't be getting the meal today.'

'Did they only feed you once a day?' asked a horrified Esther, who had caught Annabelle's whispered words.

'Yes,' she replied diffidently, 'but they didn't want us performing on full stomachs.'

'Is anyone else hungry?' Esther asked. 'Apart from Percy Enright, that is?'

Jack nodded, then asked, 'Shall I go and get Polly from the cottage?'

'I think I'm quite capable of cooking a few sausages without supervision,' Esther said. 'So if you'd all care to move to the dining room, I'll prepare a very late supper.'

As Annabelle finished off her third sausage and second slice of toast, she asked, 'Will I have to go home now?' There was something in the way she asked that pulled at Esther's heartstrings, and she shook her head.

'No,' she said, 'it's probably better if you spend the night here. There's a spare bed in Lily's room, already made up. I have to teach Primary One in the morning, so I'll take the opportunity to tell Miss Allsop that you've come to no harm.'

'Will Miss Allsop be angry with me?' Annabelle asked, apprehensively.

Esther chuckled, then reached out and tousled Annabelle's hair. 'Of course not — she'll be delighted to see you back among us. But apart from telling her, we need to keep it a secret until your parents have been informed.'

'Not to mention the police and the newspapers,' Percy muttered.

'Indeed,' Esther agreed, 'which is another reason why Annabelle had better stay here tomorrow, which is of course Friday, hidden well out of sight. Lily can stay with her, so they'll both be getting a day off school. But on Saturday we'll have to tell your parents that you're safe and well, Annabelle.'

'I suppose so,' Annabelle conceded grudgingly. 'Papa will be *so* angry with me.'

'Surely your parents will be overjoyed to learn that you've not been harmed?' Jack suggested. 'I certainly would be, if it had been Lily who went missing.'

'You're not my papa, though,' Annabelle reminded him. 'Mama will no doubt cry buckets all over me as usual, but Papa will scold me for all the trouble I've caused.'

'You weren't responsible for any of that, though, were you?' Esther reasoned.

'Not really,' Annabelle admitted. 'I was watching Lily and Caroline skipping, and feeling left out as usual, when a clown came and spoke to me from where he'd been hiding in the trees. He told me that the owner of the circus had seen me dancing when we did the Chestnut Dance in the park, and they wanted me to join their dancers straight away, but that Papa wouldn't approve, so I had to slip away there and then.'

'Someone clearly had some background knowledge of the school and its activities,' Percy muttered, only to be silenced by a meaningful glare from Esther.

'It didn't concern you, to be going against your father's wishes?' she asked.

Annabelle looked down, shamefaced. 'Papa always says that I'm no good at anything, and I had the chance to prove that I was. And I *was*, wasn't I?'

'You certainly were,' Esther assured her. 'We saw you during a Saturday afternoon performance, and that's when we realised where you'd got to. We began making plans to rescue you, because we thought you'd been taken against your will. But from what you're telling us, you went with the clown quite happily.'

'Yes, I did,' Annabelle confirmed. 'They had a coach waiting to take me to the circus, where I was shown the dance and invited to join the others. I had my own special costume — the one I'm still wearing, of course. Might I get a change of clothes, if it's not too much trouble?'

Lily was sent upstairs to find some of her spare clothing, since she was approximately the same size as Annabelle. Esther was anxious to keep her talking.

'Did they treat you well while you were there?' she asked.

Annabelle pouted. 'Until a few days ago, when they found out that somebody had come looking for me. That's when they locked me in a caravan. A horrible boy threatened to hit me if I made a sound. I wasn't so happy after that, and I think they knew, because that same boy was always hanging around, watching wherever I went. By the time Lily turned up looking for me, I was ready to leave — although I'm not looking forward to being scolded by Papa.'

'That may not happen,' Esther assured her. 'You can stay here over the weekend, at least until we've told your parents that you're safe and well, which of course we must do.'

'Can Annabelle live here, Mama?' Lily asked eagerly as she re-entered the room carrying one of her old school dresses. 'Annabelle's my friend, and I'd be happy to share my room with her.'

Esther smiled sadly. 'We'd be breaking the law if we kept Annabelle away from her parents.'

'He's not my real papa,' Annabelle declared. 'My real papa died, and Mama married my second papa because he's rich. I think he regards me as a nuisance around the house, and he's never shown me any kindness.'

'I'm sorry to hear that, Annabelle,' Esther said. 'But one more question, if I may. Was there anyone at the circus who asked you questions about the school?'

'Not that I can remember,' Annabelle replied, 'but perhaps I will tomorrow.'

'Yes, you must be very tired,' Esther conceded. 'Lily, would you take Annabelle up to your room and show her where she is to sleep?'

Once the two girls had departed, Esther, Jack and Percy sat staring at each other. Percy broke the silence.

'Clearly this was not a random kidnapping,' he observed. 'Whoever was behind it knew when Annabelle had been dancing in the park with the school, and that she was unhappy at home.'

'Lily knew that, too,' Esther replied, 'but that hardly makes her a suspect, surely?'

'It does point the finger at Annabelle's father, though,' Jack muttered. 'It's rather stretching coincidence that the girl who disappeared from the school was the same one whose father probably wants to see the back of her anyway.'

'I don't think it would be a good idea for you to accompany me when I tell Annabelle's parents that their daughter is safe and well,' Esther said.

'I don't think *you* should, either, Esther,' Percy observed. 'It's surely a job for Emily, accompanied by the man who made it all possible.'

'If you're referring to yourself,' Esther replied starchily, 'then I rather think that you're exaggerating your role in what was a team achievement.'

'I happen to agree with you there,' Percy said, 'but the parents don't know that, and I want to ask some questions of the father.'

'So you think that Mr Pickering may have been behind all this?' Esther asked.

Percy shrugged. 'Not at the very heart of it, no. But if we can shake him sufficiently, we can perhaps find out who's really behind the vendetta against the school. Now, is there any risk of a whisky and soda?'

Emily was standing outside the school's front doors the following morning, watching the pupils arriving, as Esther walked towards her with a broad smile.

'What are you looking so happy about, and where's Lily?' Emily asked.

'I'll answer both questions once we're safely out of earshot,' Esther replied. 'Come inside with me.'

Tears of relief ran down Emily's face as Esther broke the news that Annabelle was safe and well. 'We're keeping her at our house until her parents have been advised. Percy thinks that you should be the one to do that, and he wants to accompany you when you do. He's got this theory that Mr Pickering may somehow be involved.'

Emily looked shocked. 'In the abduction of his own daughter?'

'It wasn't a real abduction, as I say, but it probably suited him to have Annabelle out of the way. Percy believes that by questioning him he might acquire a lead to whoever's been trying to ruin the school.'

Emily nodded. 'If Percy wants to come along with me, then I'd be only too happy to have him by my side when I have to face Annabelle's father.'

CHAPTER THIRTEEN

'God knows it took you long enough,' Alfred Pickering complained. He looked disdainfully to where his wife had collapsed in an armchair in their sitting room, overcome by the news that Annabelle was safe and well. 'I suppose you'll be bringing her back here to explain herself?'

'She needs to rest for a day or two,' Emily said tactfully, 'and perhaps we'll summon a doctor to examine her for any possible injuries. Then we can set about having her returned to you.'

'Where she can cause more trouble, no doubt,' Pickering muttered. 'I swear I don't know what gets into that girl's head sometimes. When I was her age I set off to sea on a timber ship. I then rose through the ranks until I became captain of the *Baltic Pride*, out of Millwall, and later became the majority shareholder of the Bergen Line that owned her. I certainly didn't waste my time prancing around in a circus act! The theatres are the way to go these days, not the big top.'

'Tell us more about your commercial successes,' Percy urged him.

Pickering's chest expanded with pride as he duly obliged. 'I could see that the price of the Bergen Line shares had attained the highest point they were likely to reach, given the disruption to the timber trade as nations began competing with each other in the race for the strongest navy, so I sold out and reinvested in a variety theatre in London. They're all the rage these days, and anyone sagacious enough to have invested in them is now sitting very pretty financially, myself included. You need a clear brain and steel-like courage to play the markets these days, and

I'm fortunate to be possessed of both. Not like that addle-brained girl who calls herself my daughter.'

'Please, when can we have her back?' Lavinia Pickering asked through her tears.

'We still have a few arrangements to make,' Percy replied. 'So if you'll excuse us?'

As they walked back across Cassiobury Park, Emily looked at Percy enquiringly. 'I'm surprised that you decided to leave so quickly, Percy,' she said. 'I thought you wanted to probe deeper into Mr Pickering's possible involvement in Annabelle's disappearance?'

Percy smiled. 'He told us more than he intended, and I wanted to leave for two reasons. The first being that I didn't want you to reveal the gaffe he'd just made, and the second is that I need to head back to London to make further enquiries.'

'What gaffe?' Emily asked, her brow knitted.

Percy stopped briefly to light his pipe. He blew clouds of acrid smoke into the prevailing breeze before answering. 'You recall his reference to Annabelle wasting her talents in the big top?'

Emily clapped her hands together in realisation. 'He knew that Annabelle had been with the circus, when we'd made no mention of that!'

'Correct,' Percy replied.

'So he was involved?'

'He certainly knew where she was,' Percy confirmed. 'All I need to do now is identify Mr Pickering's contacts, and we will discover who it is who hates you so much that they want to scupper your school.'

'I suppose you'll be wanting some lunch?' Beattie Enright frowned as Percy entered the kitchen to announce his return home.

'No, I'll forswear that particular culinary challenge,' Percy told her as he leaned down to peck her cheek. 'I'm really only after a change of clothes, then I'm off out again.'

'And I'll be seeking a change of husband if you keep popping in and out like this,' Beattie complained. 'You only just caught me in, anyway. It's Saturday, and I'm midway between the vicar's weekly Bible study class and the Young Wives' Fellowship. Reverend Pointing asked if he can count on you for assistance during the Harvest Festival Fair, and I told him that I'm not even able to count on you being home these days.'

'Tell the Reverend Pointing that he can form a polite queue for my services,' Percy said with a grin. 'I'm about to unmask whoever's behind that nonsense at Esther's school.'

'How are they, anyway?' Beattie asked. 'Is there any talk of another Sunday lunch in Watford?'

'No, regrettably, since all the talk recently has been about the recovery of a girl from the school who was seemingly abducted and taken off to the circus. Except she wasn't, and we just got her back.'

'I sometimes think that I should kidnap you — that way I would at least get to see you,' Beattie muttered. 'Is it too much to hope that you'll be home for supper?'

'On that you may rely,' Percy assured her as he turned and headed for the hall.

'Where are you off to on a Saturday afternoon, anyway?' Beattie called after him.

'To see a man about a shipping line,' he replied over his shoulder as he mounted the stairs.

The head office of the Bergen Shipping Line was located halfway along the East India Dock Road, just a short walk from the railway station. Percy presented himself at the front desk, posing as a newspaper journalist wishing to research the history of the company with a view to writing a feature for *The Times* that would extol its 'magnificent contribution to the commercial success of Millwall Docks'. Within minutes he'd been supplied with the documents that he suspected would yield some interesting information.

His first check was the shareholder records, which confirmed that until two years previously, one Alfred George Pickering had held a fifty-seven per cent shareholding in the company that he'd then sold to a Stock Exchange dealer acting for an unnamed client. Percy asked for the crew lists for one of their vessels, the *Baltic Pride*, and sure enough, on a voyage to Stavanger back in 1892 it had been captained by the same Alfred George Pickering.

As he ran his finger down the crew list for that voyage, one name shone out like the beam from a lighthouse. George Walter Pilgrim of Hewett Street, Shoreditch, had been a deckhand on both the outward and return voyages, and had been discharged back in Millwall with full pay. He'd even obligingly signed for his discharge payment. Percy slipped a bribe to the young man on the enquiry desk for a copy of that particular page. He now had a copy of Pilgrim's signature, and a very good reason for pinning him up against a wall, if Miss Allsop would tolerate such an interview technique on her school premises.

'I hope you have some progress to report, since I normally enjoy a lie-in on a Sunday morning,' Emily said stiffly as she opened the door in her nightgown and overcoat in response to Percy's persistent ringing of the school's front doorbell.

'Indeed I do, dear lady, and I caught the first train out of Euston in order to tell you.'

Thirty minutes later Emily was dressed and back downstairs. She put a mug of tea in front of Percy, who was seated in the visitor's chair before the desk in her office.

'I've found a connection between Annabelle Pickering's father and the man purporting to be Stanley Pilgrim,' Percy began. 'He is, in fact, Stanley's younger brother George, and he has an unenviable reputation as a fraud artist — an unsuccessful one at that.'

'So where does that take us?' Emily asked.

'I haven't yet joined up all the dots,' Percy admitted, 'but you have to admit that it's far too convenient that Annabelle Pickering's father was once a sea captain who hired the man now installed at this school as your caretaker. You told me that George Pilgrim, as we must now call him, was already working here when you took over — might I see his references, please?'

After a good deal of time spent sorting through papers in a cupboard, Emily eventually found a creased document which she placed on the desk between them. Percy compared the signature on Pilgrim's discharge papers from the *Baltic Pride* with the reference written by the Earl of Essex for Pilgrim when he left his position as assistant groundsman to join the school, before grunting with satisfaction.

'I don't pretend to be a handwriting expert, but there would appear to be a strong similarity between the hand of George Pilgrim and the Earl of Essex,' he said. 'Is this the only reference you have?'

'So it would seem, but if the reference was supposed to have come from the Earl of Essex, then no doubt my predecessor considered it sufficient,' Emily stated. 'But Mr Pilgrim was already employed here when Annabelle disappeared, so was it a coincidence that he was able to assist in her abduction?'

'I'm not sure that he did,' Percy replied, 'but he certainly came in useful when it came to daubing ominous warnings on walls and blocking lavatories, not to mention whacking Jack — and possibly myself — over the head.'

'You believe he did that at the behest of Alfred Pickering?'

'Not necessarily,' Percy cautioned. 'I believe that both men were used by a third person who we have yet to identify — someone who has an interest in bringing down the school.'

Emily looked shocked. 'What do you intend to do with the information you have? And will the school require a new caretaker?'

'In answer to your first question,' Percy replied, 'I first of all need to confirm my suspicion that the Earl of Essex never employed a certain Stanley Pilgrim as his assistant groundsman. And in answer to your second question, almost certainly, but that can only improve the quality of the school, can it not?'

'Thank you, Percy, and please keep me advised,' Emily said. 'Now, if you'll excuse me, I have some things to do on what was supposed to be a day of rest.'

Percy arrived at the Earl of Essex's estate later that morning and immediately began to make enquiries.

'Never 'eard of the man 'til the earl give 'im casual work around the grounds,' head gardener Herbert Riddings told him. 'An' ter the best of me knowledge, we never 'ad no assistant groundsman. Not in my days anyroad, an' I bin 'ere the best part of fifteen years.'

'But Pilgrim does get casual work here occasionally?' Percy persisted.

Riddings nodded. 'So do a lot of men, an' Pilgrim's good fer fencin' an such. Not that we use 'im regular like. The last time were when the earl 'eld the fair ter celebrate the football club bein' formed.'

'When there were entertainments laid on?' Percy asked.

'Yeah, that's right,' Riddings replied.

Percy thanked him warmly for his information, then strode purposefully towards the big house.

'I'm not in the habit of hiring staff personally,' the Earl of Essex said as he sorted through the harnesses in the tack room, in search of his saddle girth. 'And I'm about to ride out with the countess, so if you'll excuse me?'

'Just one more question, then I'll leave you in peace,' Percy assured him. He extracted the reference that praised the work of one Stanley Pilgrim, assistant groundsman on the Cassiobury estate, and held it out. 'Is this your signature?'

'Good God, no!' the earl protested. 'For one thing, the school at which I was educated gave me a far better hand than that, and for another, if I'm signing anything, I simply do so with the single moniker "Essex", as is my right.'

'Thank you most sincerely,' Percy replied, 'and enjoy your ride.'

Mr Pilgrim answered the request of his employer that he report to her office, then frowned when he saw Percy already in attendance.

'What does 'e want with me?' he asked grumpily.

'The same as Miss Allsop,' Percy replied in his sternest constabulary voice. 'Namely the truth.'

'About what?'

'Well, we'll start with your real name,' Percy said.

'You know my name. It's Stanley Pilgrim.'

Percy sighed. 'I suppose that fifty per cent of the truth is a reasonable start. But it's not Stanley, is it? It's George.'

'Nah — it's Stanley.'

'Then this must be the first time I've ever conducted a conversation with a ghost,' Percy said. 'Stanley Pilgrim — your older brother, I believe — died in 1881 as the result of wounds incurred during the First Boer War. You've been impersonating him ever since, first as a wounded ex-soldier in the streets of Bethnal Green that nearly landed you a gaol term, and more recently here at Cassiobury House School, using a forged reference from the Earl of Essex.'

'Bloody lies!' Pilgrim protested, as he turned to Emily for support. 'Are yer gonna listen to all that nonsense?'

'Mr Enright has proved himself to be very reliable so far in his investigations,' Emily replied coldly, 'and the standard of your work here these past few weeks has not been up to scratch.'

'I done me best,' Pilgrim protested. 'It weren't my fault if someone took ter paintin' on yer walls, an' the lavvies got blocked, were it?'

'But it *was* your fault entirely, wasn't it?' said Percy. 'You were responsible for all those incidents that caused such inconvenience to the school, and you did so at the request — and no doubt in return for payment — of a Mr Alfred Pickering, whose daughter was recently abducted from these premises.'

'I 'ad nowt ter do with that,' Pilgrim insisted. 'An' anyroad, yer got 'er back in one piece, didn't yer?'

Percy pounced. 'How do you know that? No-one knows of the girl's successful recovery except for her parents and a few select people associated with the school — of which you are not one. Presumably Mr Pickering told you himself? Do you still deny any collusion with him?'

Pilgrim frowned. 'What collusion?'

'Conspiracy to commit abduction, which in turn means a five-year stretch in the chokey.'

At this, Pilgrim seemed to lose some of his composure. 'Look, I ain't Stanley Pilgrim, all right? I borrowed 'is name after 'e got killed, an' I admit I played the wounded soldier down the Green. But that were after I tried goin' ter sea an' found as 'ow I weren't suited to it —'

'If I might stop you there a moment,' Percy cut in. 'Would you care to tell Miss Allsop here who your captain was during your voyages on the *Baltic Pride*? You see, I know the name of the ship, which means that I also know the name of its captain in those days. So, one more confession, if you'd be so good?'

There was a brief pause while Pilgrim considered his options, which were non-existent. 'Alf Pickering,' he muttered.

'The same Alfred Pickering whose daughter Annabelle was abducted from this school?'

'Yeah, but I 'ad nowt ter do with that.'

'Aside from whacking me over the head with a club when we handed over the ransom money, not to mention doing the same to Mr Jack Enright, the husband of the deputy headmistress of this school, when he was about to discover that the so-called ghost of Lady Anne was in fact one of the clowns from Billings' Circus?'

'Will I go ter Newgate fer that?' Pilgrim asked gloomily.

Percy put on a friendly smile. 'Not necessarily. You see, I have yet to tell the local police of your involvement, and the extent to which I do that will depend on how co-operative you are with us regarding the involvement of Mr Pickering. It *was* he who paid you to vandalise the school, was it not?'

'Yeah,' Pilgrim admitted, 'but 'e always reckoned 'e were doin' it fer somebody else who was supplyin' the money. An' that same person were the one what forced 'im ter go along with 'avin' 'is own daughter kidnapped.'

'What I don't understand,' Emily interrupted, 'is how you came to become reunited with the man who'd once been your sea captain.'

'It were a coincidence,' Pilgrim explained. 'I were workin' fer the earl at the fair yer took the kids to, an' Alf Pickerin' were there with 'is missus, watchin' 'is daughter dancin'. Well, 'e come over when 'e recognised me, an' I were daft enough ter admit that I were usin' me dead bruvver's name. 'E promised not ter tell if I did summat fer 'im. That's when I took ter paintin' the walls an' blockin' the lavvies.'

'But he had no real purpose of his own to serve in getting you to do that,' said Percy, 'nor did he have any interest in having his daughter abducted. So that suggests it must all have been at the behest of a third party, does it not?'

'If yer mean there were another man involved, yeah, yer right. Pickerin' never said who that were, an' I never asked, 'cos it were none've me business.'

'Very well.' Percy looked enquiringly at Emily. 'Do you wish Mr Pilgrim to pack his bags now, or at a later date?'

Emily sighed. 'We require a caretaker at all times. Even one as bad as Mr Pilgrim.'

'And I'd prefer that he stay here, at least until we can get him to testify against Mr Pickering in exchange for a good word from me,' said Percy. He turned back to Pilgrim. 'So that will be all — for now.'

CHAPTER FOURTEEN

'Have you come to tell us when Annabelle can come home?' Lavinia Pickering asked eagerly as she rose from her deckchair on the rear lawn to meet Emily and Percy. Her husband's face was less welcoming, but he too rose, as etiquette demanded, in acknowledgement of Emily's arrival.

'It will be a few more days, but she's recovering well from her ordeal,' Emily replied.

'We just have a few more questions for Mr Pickering regarding a former maritime acquaintance of his,' Percy announced.

'And who might that be?' Pickering asked nonchalantly as he waved Percy and Emily towards two garden chairs beside a wicker table on which sat four glasses and a glass jug. 'Would you care for some lemonade?'

Emily and Percy both shook their heads.

'George Pickering,' Percy prompted, 'or Stanley Pickering, as he called himself when seeking employment at Cassiobury House School.'

'He employed a false name?' Pickering asked. 'Why would he do that?'

'Because his record as a petty criminal would have disadvantaged his application,' Percy told him. 'But you knew him by his real name, did you not?'

'Can't say that it's familiar to me,' Pickering replied airily.

'Perhaps due to the passage of time,' Percy suggested. 'Let me jog your memory. He was once a deckhand, in the days when you were captain of the *Baltic Pride*.'

'I can hardly be expected to remember the names of shipboard colleagues from eight or nine years ago, surely?'

'Eight years, to be precise,' Percy confirmed. 'But then you caught up with him at the fair hosted by the Earl of Essex in the grounds of the Cassiobury estate recently, didn't you? You were there to see your daughter perform in the dance as part of the entertainments.'

'Did he tell you that?'

'He did indeed, less than two hours ago. He also confessed to having committed certain acts of vandalism against the school, for which you paid him.'

'I rather think you should be checking with Cook, and perhaps advising her that lunch might be slightly delayed,' Pickering suggested to his wife, whose face had paled.

'I think I'd rather stay and listen to what this man has to say about your involvement with Annabelle's school,' she replied.

'They're bound to be lies,' Pickering growled.

Percy smiled. 'I haven't told you what he said yet.'

'You told us yourself that he's a criminal.'

'That doesn't necessarily alter the truth of what he said about you,' said Percy, 'specifically that you have been complicit in other events at the school, including the mysterious appearance of a ghost, and the abduction of your daughter.'

'Go inside,' Pickering commanded his wife, but she shook her head.

'I'm going nowhere if this involves Annabelle.'

'Which it does,' Emily confirmed, giving Pickering an ice-cold stare.

'Tell me, please!' Lavinia Pickering urged.

Emily turned to Percy with a raised brow. 'Do you want to be the one to tell her, or shall I?'

'Perhaps it's a matter best left to me,' Percy said, 'although I must warn you, Mrs Pickering, that you may find what you hear distressing.'

'I don't care,' Lavinia insisted. 'Just tell me, for God's sake!'

'Well,' Percy continued, 'according to Pilgrim, the choice of which child to abduct was your husband's.'

Lavinia turned an angry face towards her husband. 'Is that true, Alfred?' she demanded. 'Your own daughter?'

'She's not my daughter,' Pickering reminded her. 'And it was always guaranteed that she'd come to no harm. In fact, given her dreamy disposition, a circus was probably the best place for her. The one thing she seems capable of doing with any degree of success is dancing, so joining a dance troupe seemed like her destiny anyway. She didn't suffer any harm, as these people can no doubt confirm.'

'Perhaps *she* didn't suffer, but *I* most certainly did!' Lavinia shouted as she picked up the jug of lemonade and emptied its contents down her husband's smart blazer and slacks. 'Two weeks of mental agony, wondering what had happened to my precious child, and what she might be enduring! How could you be so heartless — so uncaring — so — so *beastly*!'

Pickering scowled as his wife stormed off across the lawn and into the house.

'It was for money, wasn't it?' Percy asked, thoroughly enjoying the turn of events.

Pickering sighed heavily. 'Yes, it was, but as I already said, the arrangement was that Annabelle was not to be harmed in any way, simply taken off to the circus and hidden away. The man who arranged for that to happen was, or so I hoped, about to invest some of his vast wealth in a new theatre that I have hopes of opening here in Watford. I'd been sweetening him up for months, and I even prevailed upon the Earl of Essex to hire him for the entertainments at that recent fair.'

'This man's name?' Percy asked.

'Beaumont,' Pickering replied. 'Henry Beaumont, the leading light in London music halls, theatres and places of popular entertainment. Every project he's touched in recent years has turned to gold, and his support alone for my proposed theatre, quite apart from any money that he could be persuaded to invest in it, would guarantee its success. So when he approached me at the fair and asked if I'd be prepared to volunteer my daughter for a fake kidnapping in which she'd come to no harm, I was only too anxious to assist. But there was no harm done, was there?'

'Did this man Beaumont say why, precisely, he wanted to stage a kidnapping of one of my pupils?' Emily asked tremulously. Percy noticed that the colour had drained from her face.

'I rather gained the impression that he had a down on the school, although he didn't say why.'

'Thank you, Mr Pickering. We'll take our leave,' said Percy. 'I take it that if called upon, you'd be prepared to tell a court what you just told us?'

'Of course,' replied Pickering, 'provided that no criminal charges will be brought against me.'

'On the assumption that this Henry Beaumont kept the five thousand pounds, I can't think of anything you might be charged with,' Percy confirmed.

Emily was silent as they walked back through Cassiobury Park. Percy waited until they were clear of the few walkers who were taking advantage of the earl's beneficence, before asking gently, 'It wasn't the school that Beaumont was targeting, was it? It was you.'

'Please,' Emily pleaded hoarsely. 'Please just leave it alone now. We've got Annabelle back, and that's all that matters.'

'What about the loss of five thousand pounds?' Percy countered. 'And who's to say that this man won't continue his sneaky attacks on your school? At the very least there must be something you can tell me that will assist in bringing Beaumont to justice. You owe it not only to the school, but to yourself.'

'I'll tell Esther,' Emily agreed in a quiet voice. 'Send her to see me this evening, and I'll tell her everything.'

Emily sat in the armchair across from where Esther was perched on the settee. 'I don't want you to get the wrong impression about me.'

Esther had accepted the invitation to meet with Emily that evening in order to acquire the information that she'd been so reluctant to share with Percy. Back at The Lodge, Esther had left Alice to put the younger children to bed, while Lily measured Annabelle for a new school dress, which she'd offered to make for her. Bertie was arranging his toy soldiers in a recreation of the English formations at the Battle of Waterloo, while Percy and Jack enjoyed a whisky and soda and took wild guesses at what Emily might be revealing to Esther.

'If it's any consolation,' Esther told Emily, 'this is by no means the first time that Percy Enright has sent me to acquire details regarding personal relationships. On one occasion I was called upon to work for a very unpleasant man who couldn't keep his hands to himself, and who'd been in an unhealthy relationship with his own sister.'

'Would you care for a sherry?' Emily asked, nervously. 'I know that I need one, and you might too, when you hear what I have to tell you.'

'I think I can guess, if it helps,' Esther replied encouragingly. 'And yes, I will have a sherry, thank you. Then you can tell me all about your previous relationship with this man Beaumont.'

Emily's eyes widened. 'What makes you think that?' she asked as she took the sherry decanter and two glasses from the sideboard.

'Because you're an attractive lady, and you've never married, as far as I know. Or were you once married to Beaumont?'

'I wish it were that simple,' Emily replied. 'But let me begin at the beginning.'

'That's always a good start,' Esther said with a smile.

'Well,' Emily began tentatively, 'you'll recall that when we first met, I told you that I was for some years a teacher at a ladies' college in Eastbourne, before becoming the principal of the teacher training college in which you enrolled?'

Esther nodded. 'I do. And thanks to you I've been able to follow the career of my dreams, for which I'll remain eternally grateful to you.'

'Well,' Emily continued, 'eleven years ago, in 1888, there was an unusual occurrence when a nine-year-old girl called Alice Davenport was enrolled into that college. She was under the temporary care of her uncle and aunt while her parents were serving in different capacities in India, and they were authorised to enrol her in the college while she was residing with them. The uncle and aunt in question were brother and sister, Henry and Adelaide Beaumont.'

'I was right, wasn't I? You did have a relationship,' Esther said, in the hope of lessening Emily's burden.

Emily grimaced. 'Right *and* wrong, as it happens.'

'Sorry,' said Esther, 'please continue.'

'Even in those days Henry Beaumont was only really interested in promoting his business interests, so Alice's care fell to her aunt, Adelaide. Adelaide was the same age as me at the time, and we were both unmarried. Adelaide made frequent visits to the school in order to enquire after Alice's progress, and it became an unspoken practice for us to meet in the private accommodation that came with my position. We became close and … and … oh, dear God, do I *have* to say it?'

'You became lovers?'

'Yes,' Emily admitted, as tears rolled down her face. Esther took out a clean handkerchief from her pocket, and handed it across to Emily.

Emily thanked Esther through her tears, then asked, 'Do you think less of me now?'

'Why should I?' asked Esther, who had never been one to observe the strict morality that seemed to govern their society.

'Because here I am, in a position of authority over young people,' Emily reminded her, 'and should any of the parents find out — well, they'd be sure to withdraw their children from the school without hesitation.'

'You're being too hard on yourself,' Esther assured her.

'It was genuine love, please believe me. I'd never had a relationship with another woman before — or since.'

Esther nodded. 'But I still don't understand why Henry Beaumont is out to ruin you. Did he resent what you meant to his sister, or did you reject his advances?'

'No, nothing like that,' Emily said quietly. 'It started to go wrong when Adelaide wanted to announce to the world that we were in love.'

'Which would have been the end of your career?'

'Precisely. I tried to plead with her not to do it, but she grew more and more insistent, and in the end I took the coward's way out and ran away.'

'You walked away from your post in Eastbourne?'

'Yes, and literally overnight. I packed up my few belongings, left a note for the headmistress telling her that I had resigned from my post, then hired a coach and returned to my parental home. I told them that I was recovering from a broken heart, and they accepted that. I thought I'd covered my tracks, but Henry Beaumont somehow discovered where my parents lived, and began sending me letters, pleading with me to return to Eastbourne. He told me that Adelaide had lost her reason following my desertion of her. I ignored all of his letters. The final letter told me that Adelaide had taken her own life. You'll never know how much the guilt has haunted me.' Emily sighed deeply. 'After eleven years I thought I'd finally put my past behind me. Then came the dreadful day of the fair in Cassiobury Park.'

'I remember now!' Esther recalled. 'We were eating ice creams when the earl came towards us with another man, and you left rather hurriedly. That other man was Henry Beaumont, wasn't it?'

'Yes, God help me,' Emily whispered as she reached for the decanter with a shaking hand. Downing half the glass in one go, she continued. 'I thought I'd given Henry the slip, but he must have somehow learned about the school.'

'I assume that Mr Beaumont recognised you, just as you'd recognised him, and decided to take revenge for what happened to his sister?'

Emily nodded. 'He certainly succeeded. I don't want the five thousand pounds back, and I don't want him prosecuted for abducting Annabelle. I just want it all to go away, so that I can get on with my life.'

Esther smiled warmly. 'Thank you for being so frank with me, Emily. With your permission, I'll just tell Percy and Jack that you had an affair with Henry Beaumont. It's no doubt what they've assumed anyway, and there's nothing to be gained by telling them the entire truth. It can remain our secret.'

When Esther reported back to an eager Percy and Jack that Beaumont was seeking revenge against Emily for a previous broken relationship, Jack was triumphant.

'For once I got it right,' he crowed.

'On that happy note, and unless supper is in immediate danger of being served, I'd better make a move towards the station, and home,' Percy declared as he rose from his chair.

Just then Alice put her head round the living room door and announced, 'The fish pie's just out of the oven, if anybody's hungry?'

'The daftest question of the week, in present company,' Percy said. 'I can always rise early and take the first train down to Euston in the morning.'

As they made appreciative inroads into the fish pie, Esther told Percy, 'Emily was most insistent that she doesn't want you to pursue Beaumont any further.'

'The bugger still has five thousand pounds of her money, which would go nicely towards my fees,' objected Percy. 'Plus, I'd hate to see him get away with all the trouble he's caused.'

'It's got nothing to do with payment for your services, or even justice for Emily,' teased Jack. 'You just don't like leaving loose ends.'

'I must say I agree with Percy,' said Esther thoughtfully. 'Apart from anything else, I'd hate to think that there could be more attacks on the school just because Beaumont thinks he can get away with it with impunity.'

'Thank you, Esther,' Percy said. 'You just gave me the justification I need to bring Henry Beaumont to book.'

'What do you have in mind?' Jack asked.

Percy shrugged. 'That will depend on what I learn about the man and his business interests. I'm sure those music halls that he owns, and which are the source of his fortune, are no better these days than they used to be in mine. Thieves, pickpockets, prostitutes — and that's just those on the stage. As for the so-called performers, there's usually one who can sing but insists on dancing, another who can dance but insists on telling jokes, and a third who's billed as a comedian but normally does little more than encourage the audience to drink more. Many a customer staggering out of one of those dens of iniquity has been robbed and left for dead.'

'So you won't be taking Aunt Beattie to one of Beaumont's music halls to celebrate your wedding anniversary?' Jack asked with a chuckle.

Percy shook his head. 'No, I will not,' he muttered. 'And I'm surprised that a woman with such refinement as Emily was ever tempted into a relationship with the likes of Beaumont.'

Esther was sorely tempted to tell Percy the truth, but remained loyal to the promise she'd given Emily. In any case, there was something else on her mind.

'Do you think we could let Annabelle return to school tomorrow?' she asked Percy.

He sighed. 'Although we now know who is behind the vandalism at the school, and no-one has any remaining reason for harming her, I'd prefer to see her kept safe until this matter has been concluded.'

'I will need to keep Lily off school as well,' Esther reminded him, 'so the sooner you blow the final whistle, the better.'

CHAPTER FIFTEEN

Esther found Emily waiting for her at the school's front doors on Monday morning, shortly before classes were due to start.

'Are you preparing to assume bell duties?' Esther asked her. 'I gather that Mr Pilgrim may not be reporting for work today.'

'He will if he wants to get paid this week,' Emily said wanly, 'and he hasn't yet been formally dismissed. I wanted to tell you about a telephone call that I received yesterday evening, from Lavinia Pickering. I assume that you've left Lily and Annabelle at home again? Perhaps that's just as well in the circumstances.'

'What did she have to say?' Esther asked, fearing that Annabelle's mother might be demanding her return to what must be an even unhappier home than it had previously been.

'She's making plans to leave her husband, and I can hardly blame her after what Percy and I learned about his involvement in Annabelle's abduction. Apparently she's going to lodge temporarily with her married sister in Cheltenham. She asked if we could look after Annabelle until she's been able to make plans to be reunited with her. She said nothing about the cost of her upkeep, I'm afraid.'

'That won't be a problem,' Esther said. 'She and Lily are close friends, and it's no hardship having her in the house. She shares a room with Lily, and can stay with us for as long as is necessary.'

Jack looked up in mild alarm as Assistant Commissioner Bruce appeared in his open doorway. The normal arrangement was for him to send for Jack if he needed to speak with him, rather than descend the three floors himself.

'Good morning, sir,' Jack said as he rose from his chair, only to be waved back down into it by Bruce. The Assistant Commissioner closed the door and slid into the visitor's chair with a conspiratorial smile.

'I need another favour from that man who isn't Percy Enright,' he admitted.

'Sir?'

'Don't pretend you don't know who I mean, Jack — the man who you can't name. I need him to finish the job he's started.'

'For the same lack of reward, you mean?' Jack felt emboldened to ask.

Bruce smiled. 'This man, whoever he is, asked originally for a thousand pounds, did he not? Well, he can have a thousand when he completes the job.'

'The job being?' Jack asked.

Bruce leaned forward and lowered his voice. 'He made a pretty good job of emptying the East End of those Russian gangs. But there's still one man left, who seemingly escaped all the mutual bloodletting, and word on the street is that he's reforming his Bessarabian mob. His name is Max Moses, and I want him taken out of the equation.'

'And you have authorisation for the payment of a thousand?' Jack asked.

Bruce nodded. 'If you name the man, I can have a draft for a thousand pounds made out in his name once the job's been done.'

'I feel obliged to tell you that the man in question is not a hired assassin,' Jack said, 'and I can't disclose his identity even for a thousand.'

'Then how will I pay him?'

'Presumably you're familiar with bearer bonds?' Jack asked. 'They're as good as cash, since they can be converted into actual money when presented at the appropriate bank. But my first reservation holds good — my contact is not a killer for hire.'

'I don't necessarily want Moses dead,' Bruce confirmed, 'just out of action on the streets of Whitechapel. I don't care how your man achieves that, but once our local people report that he's gone, then I'll hand you the bearer bond, and you can pass it on.'

'I'm normally the one who smiles when studying a menu,' Percy observed as he and Jack sat across from each other in Tang Li's Chophouse several hours later. 'So what's the good news, apart from the fact that there's meat pie available today?'

'I just negotiated a thousand-pound commission for you,' Jack told him, 'and I don't require any finder's fee, if you're paying for lunch.'

'I already did a thousand pounds' worth of work for Bruce, who then refused to pay me,' Percy grumbled. 'What does he want this time — the assassination of the Commissioner? And how will he pay me, assuming that he's not taking advantage of a man who's still wet behind the ears, even at the rank of Chief Inspector?'

'The answer to your second question is in the form of a bearer bond, which will presumably excite your interest in hearing the answer to your first question,' Jack said. It was not often that he could keep Uncle Percy in suspense, and he was enjoying himself — *and* hopefully being treated to a free lunch.

'It must be pretty important to Bruce, if he's prepared to pay the piper for once,' said Percy.

'You're presumably familiar with a man called Max Moses?'

'We're not exactly bosom companions, but I can lay claim to having once made his acquaintance. Why?'

'Bruce wants him out of the picture down in Whitechapel.'

'I'm not an assassin, nor do I have a death wish.'

'So I advised Bruce. His reply was that the thousand would become yours once Moses is gone from Whitechapel, regardless of how that's achieved.'

'Do you actually know who Max Moses *is*?' Percy asked. 'And is it meat pie for two?' he added as he saw the waiter hovering behind Jack's shoulder.

'No and yes, in that order,' Jack replied. The waiter scribbled a note on his pad and retreated towards the kitchen hatch as Jack asked, 'Moses — isn't he some sort of gang leader?'

Percy nodded. 'The worst sort, and very unforgiving. During our last encounter he offered to have my throat slit if I mentioned a word of our conversation to anyone else.'

'And you obviously didn't,' Jack said, 'so is there anything to prevent a further conversation taking place?'

'What did you have in mind?' Percy asked. 'Presumably something better than "If you would be so good as to make yourself scarce and abandon the massive criminal enterprise that you've spent years developing"? Hopefully you have something less fatal to suggest?

'*I* don't know, do I?' Jack protested. 'I'm just passing on Bruce's request.'

Their meals arrived, and they ate in silence as Percy appeared to be thinking deeply. Then, as the sound of a horn from yet another Thames tugboat drifted through the half-opened window that looked out over the Embankment, Percy gave a broad smile.

'Lunch is on me! I think I have a plan that will net me a thousand pounds.'

Before he could put his idea into action, Percy visited the London County Council offices in Spring Gardens, where, after being passed from one desk to another, he finally acquired a list of those theatres in London that were owned and operated by Beaumont Entertainments. It was an impressive number, and included some with which Percy was already familiar from his detective days with the Met, such as the Britannia in Hoxton, the Shoreditch Empire and the Royal Pavilion in Whitechapel. But the one that caught his eye was the Royal Cambridge Music Hall in Commercial Street, Shoreditch.

It had a previous existence as the Royal Cambridge Theatre of Varieties, which had burned down the previous year in circumstances suggestive of arson, either by its previous proprietor, or by Beaumont Enterprises, which had acquired the smouldering ruins at a bargain price and reopened them as the Royal Cambridge Music Hall. This gave Percy the perfect ploy for seeking an interview with Henry Beaumont, and he whistled softly to himself as he caught the horse bus down to Commercial Street.

'Mr Beaumont ain't in,' Percy was told by the burly individual smelling strongly of that day's ale, and yesterday's sweat, who stepped out in front of him and demanded to know his business as he attempted to pull open one of the glass doors at the public entrance.

'That will be a matter of serious regret to your employer,' Percy replied with an air of indifference, 'since I'm from the LCC, and I wish to be reassured that the necessary fire precautions are in place here before this evening's performance can proceed.'

'Wait 'ere, an' keep yer 'ands ter yerself,' Percy was told. Five minutes later, the man returned with an unsurprising update. 'Mr Beaumont's in now, so follow me.'

'I'm told that you're here regarding the fire regulations,' Beaumont said languidly as he looked up from the paperwork on his desk. 'In which case, you must know that we got a full clearance certificate only last week. Or are you another one seeking a backhander?'

'I'm nothing to do with the fire authorities, Mr Beaumont,' Percy said as he extracted a business card and laid it on Beaumont's desk. 'My name is Enright and I'm a private enquiry agent. Before you instruct your resident thug to throw me out, be advised that I'm here on a commission from Mr Alfred Pickering.'

'And what does *he* want?'

'His share of the five thousand, to begin with,' Percy said. 'Then he requires a monthly infusion of three hundred in cash, to be deposited to an account in his name whose details I can disclose to you once we have an agreement.'

Beaumont nodded for the resident thug to leave them. 'What five thousand?' he asked.

'Very well,' Percy replied with a sigh. 'We'll do this the hard way. I'm told that the sum of five thousand was paid over by a Miss Allsop, of Cassiobury House School, for what was intended to be the price for the release of one of her pupils who'd been allegedly kidnapped by you. Except the kidnap was a ruse, and the money was retained by you. My client is not being unreasonable in his request, given that the pupil in question was his own daughter.'

'And if I tell you what Mr Pickering can do with his attempted blackmail demand, what then?' Beaumont replied calmly.

'Then my client will advise the theatre licensing authorities of the moral character of the man who relies on his good name to keep his fleshpots in business.'

'He doesn't seriously expect me to buckle under a pathetic threat like that, does he?' Beaumont asked, faintly amused.

'He's not a man to make idle threats, Mr Beaumont. It's not really about the money, you see — it's more to do with dented pride at having been made to look stupid. It seems to me that he'd quite welcome the opportunity to drop you in it with the licensing authorities, thereby reducing your lucrative empire to a mere pile of bricks and mortar.'

'Is he prepared to negotiate the price of his silence?'

'He gave me no authority to negotiate on his behalf,' Percy replied. 'Perhaps you might want to speak with him in person. I was commissioned to deliver the message, and now that I've done so I will depart. You should also be advised that I told the sergeant behind the desk at Shoreditch Police Station that if I was not back in fifteen minutes, to send constables to enquire regarding my health.'

'Tell Pickering I'll be in touch,' Beaumont growled as he rang a small handbell on his desk. The smell of yesterday's sweat returned, and Percy hid a grin as he was shown out.

That went almost too well, he thought to himself. It needed only a telephone call to the Watford Police to complete that part of his busy afternoon schedule. Now to see a man about an escape route out of London for one of the most unpleasant men he'd ever met.

'I thought I'd seen the last of you, yer troublemaker,' Jim 'Lofty' Lofthouse complained as he peered accusingly over the bow of his two-masted fishing smack moored up alongside St John's Wharf in Wapping High Street.

'Is that any way to greet an old friend who's about to place some lucrative business in your lap?' Percy asked with a broad smile.

'Come down 'ere, where I can see yer, an' if yer've got Peelers with yer, then yer no friend've mine anymore,' Jim replied roughly.

Percy and Lofty's relationship went back some mutually beneficial years. The fishing trade was notoriously unpredictable, so it was not surprising that many of those plying their way up and down the Thames Estuary took the occasional opportunity to supplement their income with a little contraband. Cases of wine, bales of tobacco and fancy footwear out of the ports of northern Europe were one thing, but drugs, guns and people-trafficking were an entirely different matter. Lofty had, for many years, felt that the serious attention given to vessels like his by Customs and Excise, the police and the immigration authorities, was the fault of those whose cargoes were ruining it for the rest of them.

He had therefore become one of several boat owners who 'assisted' the authorities with information regarding the 'whisper' when a drugs consignment was on its way into the London Docks at the dead of night, or when a shipment of guns intended for Irish subversive elements was due to be landed on the Essex shoreline downriver. For several years he'd supplied Percy with such vital information, but there was always a risk involved, namely that the other boat owners would become suspicious if one particular vessel was never apprehended and searched. It had been Percy who had ensured that Lofty's boat was regularly intercepted and searched by police and Customs vessels, having taken care to warn Lofty in advance when this was to happen.

It was now time to call in a few favours.

'So how's tricks?' Percy asked jocularly as he warmed his hands on the cocoa mug that Lofty handed him.

'Can't complain,' Lofty replied, 'mainly 'cos no bugger listens. That said, it's got a bit trickier ever since yer moved on, an' I don't get no warning no more. So what yer doin' back down 'ere in Wappin'?'

'I have a favour to ask of you, for which you won't go unrewarded,' Percy said. 'Do you still by any chance put in at Calais or Boulogne during your extended fishing trips?'

'What yer lookin' fer?' Lofty grinned toothlessly. 'D'yer still stick that Belgian 'orse fodder in yer pipe? Or is it some brandy yer after?'

'I want you to take a friend of mine downriver tomorrow night, and across the Channel. Name your price.'

'Fer you, maybe a coupla' 'undred.'

'Make it five hundred, and his name's Max Moses,' Percy whispered, given how sound travelled across water.

Lofty's eyebrows shot up as he uttered a few profanities. 'Why are yer doin' a favour fer that scum?'

'I can't explain why,' Percy replied, 'and believe me, you wouldn't want to know. But for certain reasons Mr Moses has an urgent need to travel out of the country, and would not be best advised to do so by way of the customary channels. Hence my request that you accommodate his needs. If you can't, then I'll just move on to someone who can, but it's guaranteed money, it's clean, no-one's been tipped off, and no doubt you'll be highly regarded by Mr Moses's remaining associates here in the lower town when, and if, it comes to them turning their protection racket towards your vessel.'

'Tomorrer night, yer said? An' I can charge 'im a monkey?'

'Correct on both counts,' Percy confirmed. 'Do we have a deal?'

A quick shake of the hand and Percy climbed back onto the wharf and set off at a steady pace down Wapping High Street towards his final port of call that afternoon.

During Max Moses's first, and only, meeting with Percy, he'd been obliging enough to identify his mistress as Clara Solomons. If she was the same lady who had been running a successful upmarket brothel in Whitechapel's Ellen Street for many years, then Percy knew how he might just manage to pull off a masterpiece of deception.

He pushed open the street door to the 'Gentlemen's Club' with a nervous expression, remembering to look behind him furtively as the elegant middle-aged lady who he presumed was the proprietor demanded to know his business. 'Only you don't look the sort we normally get in here,' she added.

'I'm not,' he confirmed, 'but I need to get an urgent message to Mr Moses that it wasn't me who peached on him.'

'Which Mr Moses would that be?' she asked.

'You *are* Clara Solomons, aren't you?'

'What if I am?'

'Well, I'm told that you're the best channel of communication with Max Moses. Only I need to reassure him that it wasn't me, and that I've taken steps to ensure that he escapes. I've got a sick wife at home, you see, and I don't want there to be any misunderstanding when the authorities arrive, which is why I've arranged a swift escape out of the country for him, just to show my bona fides.'

'Are you drunk, or what?' Clara demanded, clearly confused.

Percy shook his head vigorously. 'Please, let me start again. My name is Percival and I'm a private enquiry agent. I had occasion to be of service to Mr Moses in recent weeks when I was consulted by the Home Office, who were seeking suitable persons to hand over to the Russian authorities for transportation back to Moldova. Now it seems that they have Mr Moses in their sights, and I didn't want any of his associates to blame me for it. I'm here to warn him that they're preparing to move in on him by the end of the week, and as a further sign of my genuineness I've made arrangements for him to be smuggled across to France tomorrow night.'

'We'll soon see if you're genuine.' Clara pressed a button under her reception desk. There was the distant sound of a buzzer, and two men appeared through a door to the side of the desk.

'Make sure he doesn't go anywhere,' Clara instructed the two bruisers, who each grabbed one of Percy's arms as she disappeared through the same door, reappearing a few moments later with a disgruntled-looking Moses.

'Yes, we've met before,' Moses confirmed as he glowered at Percy. 'What's all this rubbish about needing to make myself scarce?'

'It's real enough, Mr Moses,' Percy insisted as he tried to look like a man seeking to maintain his dignity whilst being terrified. 'They've sent for people from Russia to take you back there, and they'll be arriving this week. It wasn't me who tipped them off, honestly it wasn't, but I've made contact with an acquaintance who can get you safely across the Channel tomorrow night. He'll be asking for five hundred, but he's reliable, trust me. I just don't want any of your people coming after me if you get caught.'

Moses stared at him for a few moments, then nodded. 'You *look* scared enough, anyway, and maybe it's time I took a little holiday. What's this man's name, and where will I find him?'

'He calls himself Lofty and his boat's the *Canvey Princess*, moored in St John's Wharf.'

'Five hundred, you said?'

'That's what *he* said,' Percy replied. 'I didn't want to haggle, in the circumstances.'

'Maybe I'll haggle for myself.' Moses grinned unpleasantly. 'Tell your man Lofty to expect me after dark tomorrow night — say nine o'clock. As for you, Mr Percival, I'll leave word that you're not to be harmed. Now get out while I'm still feeling generous.'

Back out on the street, Percy took a deep breath and reflected that, all things considered, spying on errant husbands had a lot to recommend it.

CHAPTER SIXTEEN

The following morning, Percy was barely behind his desk in the Devonshire Street office when he received a telephone call from Inspector Bradbury at Watford Police Station.

'Many thanks for your tip-off,' said the inspector down a crackly line. 'We kept an eye on the Pickering house, as you suggested, and shortly before ten o'clock yesterday evening we intercepted a man armed with a shotgun climbing through a side window that he'd just broken. Mr Pickering was unharmed, and the man we intercepted, who gave the name "Quigley", admitted to having been paid to kill Mr Pickering by one Henry Beaumont, who was arrested at his place of business in Whitechapel about an hour ago. But there's something else to report that you probably *weren't* expecting.'

'Go on,' Percy invited him.

'As is routine in such matters, we insisted on searching the Pickering house for other possible intruders, despite Mr Pickering's protests. During the search we discovered the body of a woman hidden under a bed on the first floor of the property. She'd been strangled to death. Pickering admitted to having carried out that act in a blind rage after the lady in question, who proved to be his wife, had declared that she was leaving him. He's being held in a local cell until we can send him down to Pentonville to await trial at the next Assizes.'

Percy put in a call to Jack, and they agreed to meet for lunch later that day.

'Tell Bruce to have his thousand ready by the end of the week,' Percy said when he and Jack were seated at Tang Li's. 'I'll contact you again by phone later in the week and get you to check with our contacts across the Channel that Max Moses has left London in the belief that he was about to be deported back to Russia.'

'You took a serious risk,' Jack observed after Percy explained how he'd brought that about.

Percy nodded. 'Which is why Bruce had better keep his end of the bargain, or I'll do the trick in reverse, and convince Moses to return.'

'I'm still getting over what you told me about the Pickerings,' Jack muttered. 'And it's a pity you couldn't get Emily's five thousand back before Beaumont was locked away on a conspiracy to murder charge.'

'Emily just wanted the entire business to end,' Percy reminded him. 'With Beaumont either serving life in prison, or possibly even taking the drop, he can't be of any further annoyance to her. I just hope that she wasn't still holding a torch for him, that's all.'

'From what Esther has told us, I believe that particular torch to have been long since extinguished,' Jack commented.

Percy waited a couple of days before taking the horse bus down to Wapping. He strolled casually down the High Street until he reached the basin that contained St John's Wharf, and looked anxiously over the wall. Sure enough, the *Canvey Princess* was tied up back at her mooring, and he sat on her gunnels until he saw movement inside the cabin. He waved to Lofty, who emerged onto the open deck with a broad smile.

'Thanks fer that, Mister Enright,' the sailor said with a grin. 'That were the easiest monkey I ever made, an' I got some of that baccy that yer like, as a thank you.'

'You delivered your passenger without any problems?' Percy asked.

Lofty nodded. 'Calais Harbour, on a fallin' tide, so I didn't 'ave long ter stay there, once I'd grabbed yer that baccy from the chandler's shop. I got me monkey, no problem, but 'e were a surly bugger.'

'He'd be even more surly if he knew I'd tricked him,' Percy said with a chuckle. He waved Lofty farewell as he headed off to send a telegraph from the harbourmaster's office to Scotland Yard's International Detachment in Calais, requesting that they confirm, to Assistant Commissioner Bruce, that a man called Max Moses could be found in their immediate location.

On Thursday morning Percy received the anticipated telephone call from Jack.

'I've got a thousand reasons why you're buying me lunch again, Uncle,' he said down the line. They again arranged to meet for lunch at Tang Li's Chophouse later that day.

'I still can't believe how you achieved the almost impossible,' Jack said admiringly as he handed over the bearer bond and opted for lamb chops. Percy gave a chuckle, partly because there was meat pie on the menu again, and partly because Bruce had finally come good on his promise.

'It was all too easy, as it always is when you take the trouble to identify your quarry's greatest weakness. Moses was terrified of being returned to Moldova.'

'What's *my* greatest weakness?' asked Jack.

Percy thought for a moment before answering. 'You have two,' he told Jack. 'The first is your very laudable love for Esther and your children. I could, were I a villain, always get to you by threatening to harm them.'

'And the second?'

'Your naive honesty,' Percy said mischievously. 'You came all the way down here with a bearer bond for a grand without calling in at the bank on which it's drawn and pocketing it, then pretending that Bruce refused to pay.'

'I admit that I am an honest fellow,' Jack conceded. 'But what grounds do you have for claiming that I am naive?'

'Your belief that I'm going to be paying for this lunch,' Percy chortled.

On Saturday they held a celebration lunch at The Lodge. As they tucked into the roast beef that Jack had carved with pride, Emily placed a tin of Percy's favourite pipe tobacco in front of him before kissing him on the cheek.

'I'm afraid that's all I can give you at the moment, apart from my heartfelt thanks. The loss of five thousand pounds quite wiped me out financially, so your fee will have to wait until next term's fees start rolling in. The good news is that, thanks to you, there will be more pupils. Ever since that wonderful newspaper story about how the school rallied round to rescue Annabelle, my phone has barely stopped ringing with calls from the parents of prospective students.'

Percy smiled. 'The man from *The Times* owed me a favour. But out of interest, how much *are* your fees?'

'Slightly over a hundred pounds a term,' Emily replied. 'Why?'

'Did we ever agree what my fee was to be? In fact, was it ever agreed that I'd be charging you anything at all?'

'Not as such, no,' Emily conceded. 'But I approached you on a commercial basis before I learned of your family connection with Esther, and so it must be assumed that there will be a fee payable.'

'Well, let me see,' Percy said. 'I believe that Annabelle is eight years old, am I right?'

'Yes, but what does she have to do with it?' Emily asked.

'If she were to stay on at your school until the legal leaving age of eleven, that would involve, what, nine terms?'

'Yes, but —'

'Nine hundred pounds in total?'

'A little over that, actually, but —'

He raised his hand to cut off the rest of her reply. 'My fee just became a thousand pounds, all of it commuted into free tuition for Annabelle for the remainder of her school life.'

There was an amazed silence, broken by Jack. 'That's *so* generous of you, Uncle.'

Percy smiled. 'Not really, when you think about it. I was recently given a thousand pounds by an assistant commissioner at Scotland Yard who's probably having trouble sleeping at night thinking about who it went to. More to the point, has it not occurred to you all that Annabelle is now an orphan? Jack and Esther have very kindly taken her in, but they can hardly be expected to pay her school fees. It's one of the great regrets of my life that Beattie and I never had children, which is partly why we were happy to provide a home for Jack when my brother died. That worked out reasonably well, I think you'll agree, so let's see if the Enright magic can work for another young person.'

It fell silent again, until Esther spoke. 'If ever again I'm tempted to be critical of Percy Enright, I wish to have it on record that as of this moment I think he's the most wonderful person that God ever put on this earth.'

Percy grinned and turned towards Emily. 'Do you by any chance have pen and paper? I'd like that recorded, if you'd be so good.'

A NOTE TO THE READER

Dear Reader,

I hope you enjoyed reading this latest instalment in the Esther and Jack Enright Mystery series, and I hope that it lived up to your expectations.

Much has happened in the years since Jack and Esther first met, when Jack was a young police constable patrolling his beat through the dark and dangerous byways of Whitechapel, and Esther was an orphaned seamstress living in a single room in a Spitalfields lodging house. Fate brought them together when Jack the Ripper weaved his web of fear in London's East End, and they are now living in middle-class comfort in a Hertfordshire market town. Jack is enjoying a senior desk job in Scotland Yard that keeps him away from the dangers of uniformed policing on the streets, while Esther lives out her dream of being a teacher in a private school.

They are on the right side of a social divide that was to persist for another generation, before the Great War proved to be a social leveller that finally recognised the dignity and worth of the ordinary man, and demonstrated through necessity that women had a more worthwhile role to play in the workforce. For the moment they are each playing a role in the dying days of Victoria's reign, unaware of the massive social upheavals that will shortly change England beyond recognition.

Cassiobury House School, of which Esther is the deputy headmistress, is of course fictitious, but it is symbolic and typical of that era. Education at that time was compulsory for all children aged between five and eleven, but its availability and quality varied enormously according to one's wealth. The

Board Schools that provided free education for the working classes were no better than the efforts of dedicated individuals who did their best (as they do even today) with the limited resources available to them, while the upper classes sought to keep the class divide as wide as possible with the public schools that provided the nation with its future leaders at a prohibitive price in school fees.

Between the two were the private schools such as Cassiobury House, to which middle-class parents paid relatively modest fees to ensure that their offspring acquired an education sufficient to gain them entry into the same professions that provided their parents with their incomes — provided, of course, that they were male, because it would be another generation before most of the professions were open to women.

Jack and Esther can surely be forgiven their satisfaction at having made it into the comfort of this 'middle class'. Jack is now safely behind a desk, and no doubt examining his conscience as he sends recruits into the poverty-stricken and potentially lethal warrens of those parts of London that have been overtaken by criminal gangs, while Esther can recall the days when the view from her solitary window on the upper floor of an East End tenement was a cat food preparation yard; today, several of the windows of The Lodge in which she and her family reside with their two domestic servants look out over the verdant pastures of Cassiobury Park.

Those familiar with Watford will know that park as a public space which has been in existence since 1909, when it was purchased by Watford Borough Council from the estate of the Earldom of Essex. In 1927 the council undertook the demolition of Cassiobury House itself, but in the year covered by this novel it was a classic example of an English estate being held together by money that came from a strategic wedding between the latest in a long line of peers of the realm and an American heiress happy to become an English titled lady. The 7th Earl of Essex seems to have been as community-minded as suggested in the story, and contemporary supporters of Watford FC can indeed thank him for his early interest in seeing professional soccer established in his neck of the woods, if only to provide rigorous exercise for the 'lads' he hoped to recruit into the local yeomanry force in which he served as a major.

The Bessarabian Tigers, also known as the 'Stop At Nothing Gang', were described by a police inspector based in the East End at the time as 'the greatest menace ever known to London'. Max Moses really existed, and was obliged to leave the country in a hurry after he killed a member of the rival Odessians. I used his hasty departure as a convenient literary opportunity for one of Percy's 'schemes', and although it was not uncommon for the Bessarabians to fight with their rival Odessians, to their immediate north in Bethnal Green, the turf war sparked by Percy was another piece of literary licence on my part. The move to the United States allowed Moses to shake off his murky past, and after service in that nation's forces in the First World War, he launched a Hollywood acting career.

While Moses was abroad, another First World War veteran began to rise through the ranks of the Bessarabian Tigers. His name was Alfred 'Alfie' Solomon, the real-life inspiration behind the character Alfie Solomons in the television series *Peaky Blinders*.

The shoplifters who plagued the West End department stores operated precisely as described, and were a menace to the rapidly developing emporia lining Oxford Street and Bond

Street at the time. To combat this worrying development, the leading retail stores began to employ individuals known variously as 'Asset Protection Investigators', 'Undercover Shoppers' or 'Loss Prevention Detectives', and the store detective was born. Once again I used literary licence to credit Percy Enright with the creation of this novel form of crime-fighting.

Percy has, of course, retired as a serving police officer. However, like many in his position, he has employed his acquired skills in the course of a new career in the private sector. There was a ready market for those skills among those well-placed members of society who wished to keep certain matters discreet. The obvious context for this was, of course, the unmasking of marital infidelity, and it was possible to make a steady living out of matters that ended in the divorce courts. However, as recorded here, only husbands could bring such proceedings in respect of their wives' adultery at the time. It would require legislation passed in 1923 to redress this imbalance.

Although it no longer exists, the Royal Cambridge Theatre of Varieties at 136 Commercial Street, Shoreditch was, in its day, typical of the somewhat 'downmarket' entertainment venues known as 'theatres of varieties' or 'music halls'. Audiences were able, and indeed encouraged, to consume alcohol 'in house' while a smorgasbord of dubious 'artistes' paraded across the stage in various states of undress, telling risqué jokes or offering acrobatic displays, all of which were introduced by a master of ceremonies. Fire destroyed the original Royal Cambridge Theatre of Varieties in 1896, but such was the money to be made from this branch of the performing arts that it reopened only two years later as the Royal Cambridge Music Hall, and as such it was a fitting enterprise to place in the fictional hands of Henry Beaumont, an exemplar of the theatre proprietors of that era.

Likewise, Petticoat Lane, as it is now known, has a far from salubrious history. Located in Spitalfields, it consists today of two distinct markets, one on Wentworth Street and the other on Middlesex Street, and dates back as far as the seventeenth century. By the time of this novel, it was well known to the Metropolitan Police's H Division as the haunt of criminals and the hub of many suspicious activities. It was said that you could expect someone to steal your petticoat at one end of the market and then sell it back to you at the other end. It was the first choice of 'fences' who would buy stolen goods from criminals before selling them in their shops or on stalls. One of the most notorious of these fences, Isaac Solomon, is said to have served as the inspiration for Dickens's character Fagin.

Sexual relationships between women were by no means unheard of, and were almost a natural development from those female friendships in Victorian England that were often over-romanticised. It was not until some women began to assert their individuality, and demand recognition, that those who felt threatened by such freedom of expression began to allege that some so-called 'friendships' were more than that. Once 'outed', the more militant of those who had formed same-sex relationships demanded their own recognition.

The census commenced in 1801, and was conducted every ten years with the purpose of measuring community demographics and assessing the resources that it would need for the next decade. It was the change in the occupancy of the Hewett Street residence between the 1881 and 1891 censuses that enabled Percy to investigate the possibility that George Pilgrim was impersonating his dead brother Stanley.

So what awaits the Enrights now? Can they finally relax in their middle-class comfort and forget all the traumas that they've endured on the way? Unfortunately, the nation will shortly experience a massive upheaval at the very summit of public life that will have implications for them all. Queen Victoria will die in 1901, to be succeeded by her son and heir, Prince Albert ('Bertie') Edward as Edward VII.

The funeral of one monarch, and the coronation of another, will place huge strains on an undermanned Metropolitan Police Force, requiring Jack to work night and day in order to stretch the 'thin blue line' as far as it will reach, and ensure the people's safety as they spill onto the streets to watch both public spectacles. Then the soon-to-be-crowned monarch will become the chief suspect in a murder that occurred behind the walls of Marlborough House. Read all about it in the next novel in the series, *The Belvedere Scandal*.

As ever, I would be delighted to see a review of my book posted on **Amazon** or **Goodreads**. Alternatively, feel free to visit, and contact me on, my author website: **davidfieldauthor.com**.

Happy reading!

David

Sapere Books is an exciting new publisher of brilliant fiction and popular history.

To find out more about our latest releases and our monthly bargain books visit our website:
saperebooks.com

Printed in Dunstable, United Kingdom

63909688R00099